D0581193
Books ar
the last date below.
APR 2008
5 NOV 2008
27 JUN 2012
06 SEP 2012
Williams

LAWSON LIBRARY
R39097F0121

Other titles from Hodder Children's Books

Incarceron
The Oracle
The Archon
The Scarab
The Lammas Field
Darkwater Hall
Catherine Fisher

Cherry Heaven
The Diary of Pelly D
L. J. Adlington

Door of No Return
Sarah Mussi

JUPITER
Williams

S. I. MARTIN

Hodder Children's Books
A division of Hachette Children's Books

First published in Great Britain in 2007
by Hodder Children's Books

1

A Catalogue record for this book is available
from the British Library

ISBN-13: 978 0 340 944066 6

Typeset in Berkeley by Avon DataSet Ltd,
Bidford on Avon, Warwickshire

Printed in the UK by CPI Bookmarque, Croydon, CR0 4TD

The paper and board used in this paperback by Hodder Children's
Books are natural recyclable products made from wood grown in
sustainable forests. The manufacturing processes conform to the
environmental regulations of the country of origin.

Hodder Children's Books
a division of Hachette Children's Books
338 Euston Road, London NW1 3BH
An Hachette Livre UK Company

To the three Ws

[1]

There was a parcel of bonga in the cold store, after all. Mr Unwin had lied. So we took it. We could hear Mr Unwin snoring as we felt our way back to the dormitory through pitch-black corridors. The three of us moved quickly but carefully. Beneath our bare feet, ice was forming on the flagstones.

William Tamba led the way. He was shivering very badly. I should never have asked him to come, really. It is well known that the African-born perform poorly in cold weather. He sweats most disgracefully throughout the school day, and is incapable of stopping his teeth from chattering. I have tried to speak to his brother about him on several occasions as his behaviour brings shame on all of our race (especially on public outings) but I fear his brother is now an imbecile, having lost his mind since first setting foot in England. Or perhaps he was an imbecile before he left home. I don't know. It is said the family hails from Bumpe or Tikonko, or somewhere very far inland, upriver and pagan.

There was William Tamba, William Thorp and me.

We passed the fat brown-paper package between us, taking sniffs and giggling as the powerful scent of smoked fish filled the dark spaces of the academy.

Will Thorp ran ahead, eased open the courtyard door and led us along shadowed walls into the dormitory. I was glad a member of the Thorp clan was with me. They are good people and he is worthy of them. Of all people, my father is most fond of the Maroons. Like most Jamaicans, Master Thorp, though young, is very versatile and determined. Perhaps they are the best of our people in Sierra Leone, though I fear the worst if they rise to governance. They would create a military state where Christ's word would go unpreached and the English who live among us would be put to death by the sword, to be sure. And that would not do at all.

A low cheer rolled towards us from the unlit room. I could feel the expectation mounting as I lit my tiny lantern, and bodies shuffled from their bunks to surround me in the gloom. I patted the bunk above my own and shook my brother, Robert. He could sleep through Our Lord's Second Coming.

'Gentlemen!' I held high the parcel. 'I bring bonga!'

My friends went wild. They jigged and bounced about the room as silently as they could. Some of them (having no nightclothes) wear the same items day and night, saving only the collars and cuffs to wash. A greater number still (I among them) spend the night swaddled in three or more heavy blankets as well as proper cotton nightshirts and a towel or two about our heads like old maids at Northcote Road Market.

London is cold.

'Look, look here.' I turned the parcel's worded side for all to see. 'It's from Mrs Perth, Susan's mother. I knew she hadn't forgotten us! See the seal and stamp of her shop?'

'So there really was a present for us,' Robert squealed. 'And Mr Unwin stole it. And he lied! He lied!'

I feared he was on the verge of tears. I moved to console him as another voice declaimed, 'We will divide the food now.' I knew that voice – and everyone knew what it meant by 'we'. The Caulkers. There were three of them at the academy. All as tall as they were evil. Their family were pirates, slave traders and idolaters who owned the Banana Islands off the coast of Sierra Leone. Although they were as black as any of us, in fact blacker than some, they were said to be the descendants of an Englishman who'd settled upcountry and married into local royalty two centuries before. John Caulker pushed his way towards me, brandishing a small machete. We knew that his brothers, situated at other points in the room, would be similarly armed.

I threw the package at his feet. He ripped it open and chopped the dried fish with surprisingly judicious strokes. He threw me a fish head. I passed it to Robert.

'Line up and receive from me!' he commanded the others. 'You may eat now or save your share for soup,' he added unnecesarily.

The Jamaicans (who love dried fish almost as much as they do peppers) were the first to finish. They sat and watched the rest of us like dogs. We Nova Scotia boys agreed to eat half now and pool the remainder for a Sunday stew. All the African-born (after taking a discreet nibble here and there) handed their share to the Caulkers and returned to their beds.

I was woken by my brother tugging at my shoulder. He was moaning and appeared unable to talk. 'What is it, Robert? Speak.' He groaned all the more deeply. From all sides now I could discern similar sounds, and worse, wet burps, wetter farts, and splashes.

'Robert?' I felt for his face. His cheeks ballooned. The mind of man is remarkable in its recognition of and reaction to the presence of danger, but I was not fast enough to evade the first jet of vomit and it shot against my ear as I turned away all too late. Robert howled like a demon and produced a second and a third stream. A splatterfall on the floor added to a rising stench in the room, confirming that his body was expelling the evil from both exits. But I could not help him for already I could feel my own bowels bubble and tighten before rocketing their addition to the noxious effluent pooling the room.

All around the room, those that could had lit their lanterns. I wish they had not. It was a scene from hell. Writhing half in and half out of our bunks, some of us spinning on the floor like tops, all who had eaten of Mrs Perth's fish were doubly spraying.

We cried. Cried for the wasted fish, cried for our sweating sickness in that unheated winter room, we cried for our mothers far off in Africa. And we cried because footsteps from the corridor, staggered clomping footsteps, were getting closer . . . and we all knew what that would bring. Mr Unwin.

He stood illuminated in the doorway. Black nightshirt, blue chin, double candlestick and black hat. 'Ye filthy animals!' he roared in a voice strangely big for his body. He pinched his nostrils and staggered back. 'Accursed race! Have you no shame? Cleanse yourselves, O sons of Africa! Be cleansed!' He flung his hands at us like a conjuror seeking to banish us from sight and memory. He screamed for the house-servants, 'Mary, Maggie, bring water, brushes and mops aplenty. Fever's afoot! Hurry now!' Unwin stood there scrutinizing us as a watcher of the skies through an eyeglass spies a new and baleful star.

I heard the clang and splish of full water buckets left outside our door. 'You'll clean yourselves. This is no work for good Christian women. A thief abides amongst ye and on the morrow one of you will pay dearly for this infraction.' His stare rested on each of us for a moment longer than was comfortable.

Seven thousand and two hundred seconds passed before our stomachs and bowels were truly voided of the poison. We set to work – that is to say, everyone except the Caulkers, myself and Robert. The Caulkers paid Henry Fantimance and Adam Naimbana to clean for them. I don't remember who cleaned for us but they were paid at a better rate, I'm sure. The proper rate for their labour, as is our family way. So well were they paid that Robert and I even had clean, dry linen to wear when we arose for church later that morning.

We marched in silence across Clapham Common.

We knew one or more of us would suffer a beating tomorrow for last night's antics. I sought to raise our spirits by mocking William Tamba. The day before, while playing a ball game, he claimed to have seen a black man in the bushes beyond the ponds when he went to retrieve a lost ball. Apparently, the fellow was just crouching down in the bushes with the ball. He spoke Mande to him as well as English.

'Where was your mad Mande man again, William?' I began.

'There was a man over there.' He pointed vaguely at a line of bushes nearby.

'A man?'

'He was talking to me.'

'Talking to you, eh?'

'Yes, in Mande language.'

'A Mande-speaking man in Clapham?'

'He was a black man from our country. He was watching us play football.'

'Where is he, then?' I pretended to scan the horizon. 'Where is this strange fellow?'

'He passed me the ball and said hello to me. In Mande language. He has gone away now.'

'Back to Sierra Leone, yes?'

'No, back to the bushes.'

I patted his face and went back to my place in the line.

'We'll look for him after church, shall we? I feel we need more black people in this sad little village, don't you?' I said loudly.

Everyone cheered at that until we were ordered to be silent and remember we represented the school.

I believe the English dislike worship. They spend so little time in the house of the Lord. Back home everyone (except some Maroon folk, of course) can be found in church all day every Sunday giving thanks and praise to the point of exhaustion. Here the practice is to pass less than two hours in the company of the Most High. It is a wonder they are so blessed.

But we too are blessed. We owe our family's survival and success not just to frugality, industry and thrift, but above all to the intervention of Our Lord. I prayed then: for Mother and Father, that their businesses may prosper and Father's ministry continue. I gave thanks for the courage and fortitude that led them out of slavery to claim their freedom, first in icy Canada where I was born, then back to our African motherland from whence we were so brutally torn. I offered a prayer for His Majesty, the King. Long may his wise counsel prevail. Prayers were also due to the rector of this church, Reverend Venn, and others in the congregation – Mr Wilberforce and Mr Macaulay – who agitate in places of influence for the freedom of our people. I prayed for our young ladies out of sight. (I could hear them singing in the upper gallery, their voices clearer and richer than the white people. Or perhaps they, like we, sang loudly to keep warm.) We see very little of them now they receive education at Battersea Rise. It is as if we are deliberately kept apart, which is a shame as Susan is the daughter of Mary Perth, one of our leading citizens and our bonga benefactress. The other girls are from the interior.

For Mr Unwin I invoked a curse. His beery breath rolled over my shoulder carrying slurred words and Northland intonations. I asked that his punishment tomorrow would not fall too heavily upon the younger boys who fear him. He is an ugly man with no love for our young people. Death will come for him soon. Of this I am certain.

I fashioned a second curse, this time for the shopkeepers of Camberwell who supplied the crowd in that dreadful village with rotten fruit to hurl at us as we attended St Giles' church a week ago today. Some of the English are lower than animals. Guests in our country would never be treated in such a manner.

All too soon, with barely time for some scant and insincere readings and teachings, we were back outside in the fresh, frosty air of the Common.

The London newsheets report that our presence in this parish has increased the congregation tenfold. I can believe this. Reverend Venn is a clever, but uninspiring preacher and upon our arrival some years ago there were seldom more than two score men and women in attendance. Now I regularly count above one hundred and forty heads, most of them are outsiders, totally unknown to me. Some arrive with sketchpads. They while away the sermons rendering our African profiles. Others elect to be seated in proximity to us. They beam. I hear say there is a market in such pews.

There is never enough time to pray as I would like. Never time to pray for everyone. As usual I was silent as we marched in ranks back to the academy. This was when I offered my final prayer every Sunday. The prayer I could never mouth in any church. I prayed for our dear departed brother, Patrick. Brave, tender, clever Patrick, who was taken from us at such an early age. I know he cannot be made flesh again so I ask God for a vision, or a dream, of how it would be if the three of us – Patrick, Robert and me – were students here together. Three brothers strong. Like the Caulkers. But just two of us walk this earth, and so it must remain.

Because I killed Patrick. In anger.

[2]

London, 16th January 1800

My dearest Father,
I trust this letter finds you in the best of health. I am given to understand that your Christian missions upriver are flourishing and that your timber business continues to forge links of commerce between our country and this. All of us here get regular news about home from Robert. I do believe he has spent the larger part of his money on newspapers and correspondence from all quarters of the globe. He seems to have the news of the world at his fingertips and he brings us much joy, although his choice of companions leaves much to be desired and causes me to wish he would devote more attention to human nature rather than printed matter. Lately he has befriended the mad Tamba boy, William (who has taken to imagining a strange black man lurking in the bushes around the school – speaking Mande, apparently). Moreover, he has accepted an invitation to accompany him to dine at the home of Sir Thomas Manton at Stratford. Sir Thomas is a

spice and wood importer. His influence, I fear, may be disadvantageous to our own family's enterprises along the Rio Pongo. I will accompany Robert on this journey to ensure he does nothing to disgrace the family or imperil our prospects. This is a strange country. Here a fool like William, who cannot even spoon soup correctly, is addressed as 'Your Highness' simply on account of his father being a chief, whereas those like ourselves who have little land, but are schooled in all the social graces are treated as commoners. Very odd.

It is my unfortunate duty to report that yesterday afternoon the entire school was assembled for the funeral of one of our classmates. (Measles again.) I cannot remember his name. He must have been from a native family. Had he been Maroon or Nova Scotian he would have been known to us. I doubt I ever spoke more than two words to the fellow, even on the voyage to England, but I believe Robert made a playmate of him for a short while. There have been far too many funerals of our young people in this parish during our short sojourn in this country.

For the first time at a funeral here, even though the deceased was largely unknown to me, I cried. Robert also cried. I believe his tears were not for yet another young African being covered with grey English soil, but were in memory of the day six years ago when we finally laid our

Patrick to rest. My tears were, of course, for Mother; the mother that Robert never knew. She who died giving birth to him. My abiding consolation is that she lived long enough to take her last breath under African skies.

Robert and I continue to enjoy robust health despite the sickness all around us and the bitter cold and damp which the weak fires in this school do little to allay. We have to hammer through the ice in the water buckets in order to have our morning wash. This constant frost is severe and it reminds me of the tales you told us about your sufferings throughout those long, atrocious American winters. Even though I was very young, it may be that I still carry some memory of that experience in my blood, for of all the boys here, the cold seems to affect me the least. I believe the wintry weather is in fact doing us good and that it hardens us for the trials that leadership of Sierra Leone shall demand of us.

I will take my leave from letter-writing now, Father, as the bell has been rung for supper. I will endeavour to encourage Robert to put pen to paper some time in the next few days. Until then, I leave you in the care of Our Lord Jesus Christ until we meet again.

Your loving son,
Jupiter

[3]

The ingenuity of Mr Unwin's sadism was boundless. He had left all the windows in the building open to 'air the house', and in place of the classroom's usual heavy damp chill, we shivered over our desks in our topcoats in the wild ice-laden draught he would describe as 'bracing'. We stood to greet him as he entered.

'Be seated. I will now ask the thief to present himself for punishment. Reveal yourself!'

No one moved. We sat as rigidly as we could, blinking like soldiers on parade. The Yorkshireman hopped around his desk and grabbed the oldest Caulker boy by the ear. 'Are you our midnight marauder, Albert Caulker?' He twisted the ear, pulling Albert's head round with it. 'Is it you, eh? You and your thieving band of brothers!'

Albert moaned. The only other sound was the chattering of William Tamba's teeth. We froze. In a flash the schoolmaster appeared behind him and cuffed the back of his head twice for no good reason.

But William was not his target that Monday

morning. He stopped before Robert's desk. 'So. Who stole the bonga?' When he cleared his throat we cringed. We knew what was coming. 'Me seh, a who deh tief tief de bonga?'

It is always hilarious when white people talk the way they believe our people do. Some of them, like Mr Macaulay, who lived with us in Africa, do it quite well, but it's still funny. Others, like Mr Unwin and a couple of the odder housemaids (who never saw black people in the flesh before meeting us), for some reason tend to adopt this behaviour as a prelude to either violence or vile affections. Unlike the servants, we know Unwin has learnt all he knows from a Creole dictionary and grammar he hides under his bed.

'Who tief de good good bonga? A yu?' He crouched down to glare at Robert. To his credit, my little brother remained motionless, though his cheeks quivered with suppressed laughter.

'Is laugh yu deh laugh, eee?' He crouched closer, still waiting for mirth to erupt. Robert did not oblige him. Unwin marched back to his desk and extracted the cane. 'I will thrash each of you in turn until the thief and liar presents himself. You have one final chance.'

Silence reigned. 'Very well. Robert Williams, step forward!' He cut air twice with the cane. 'From laughter to tears is but a short journey. Bend over, boy.'

'You will not touch him!' The voice that boomed from my body surprised me. It was my father's voice. 'You will not touch him, Mr Unwin. Robert, remain at your desk!'

I strode across to stand before the teacher. I dwarfed him. 'I stole the fish. If anyone will be punished, it will be me. Thrash on, Mr Unwin.'

Have you ever had a play fight with a younger brother or sister? I mean a brother or sister almost half your age and size? Well, you know there always comes a time when you allow them to land a punch just so they can keep their dignity, even if they started it in the first place? Well, being thrashed by Mr Unwin was like that. Blow after blow of the cane fell into empty space as I stepped aside and dipped away. Unable to hit any part of my body directly, he went wild and charged at me using the cane like a sword. So I stood still to allow him his dignity-strike. The tip of the cane jabbed my shoulder just above my armpit. Frankly, I've felt more pain from picking my nostrils.

The whole class laughed. I tried not to join them. Unwin was now face-to-face with me, shrieking like a lunatic and working the cane against me from side to side like a machete on an unyielding stalk. I collapsed with laughter. I rolled about the floor, my face now so wet with tears that it was a while before I realized he was trying to kick me. Have you ever been kicked by a dog? That was how it felt to be kicked by Mr Unwin. The drunkard was so unaccustomed to moving his leg joints through any arcs that he had to push his rigid leg from his waist and lower back. I can only imagine it looked odder than it felt because by now all my classmates were standing on their desks or running around the room or, like me, rolling about on the floor laughing like hyenas.

Then he caught me hard in the face with the cane. Twice. In a single rage-powered movement I was on my feet in the boxing stance my father taught me and my left fist was in his belly, closely followed by my right into the bridge of his nose. He crumpled. I stood over him, willing him to stand again so I could pummel him anew. Only the presence of the Caulkers holding me back stopped me from murdering him that morning.

Unable to either stand or catch his breath, the teacher crawled from the room on all fours. As he reached the door he turned and rasped at me, 'I'll break you, break you and bring you down to the slave and son of slaves that you are, Jupiter Williams!' He turned to the class. 'I'll break you all!'

My fellow pupils cheered me and slapped me on the back. I was their champion.

I straightened my clothes.

I closed the classroom window.

[4]

'. . . and yet by all accounts, he is an outstanding scholar, one of the most able, nearly as gifted as his brother,' whispered Mr Sharp to Reverend Venn.

'From one of the very best families as well –' Mr Stephen consulted a sheaf of notes '– spreading the light of the Gospels and commerce throughout the most inhospitable regions of that dreadful land.'

'They are well connected over here too. His father visits London occasionally and is received in the highest circles. He is a close friend of the authorities in Freetown and is no stranger to the school's governors. I understand he hopes for a place at Oxford or Cambridge for the younger boy.'

They spoke about me as if I wasn't standing in the room before them. But I didn't care. I was warm. A magnificent fire warmed the back of my legs. I stared above the heads of the three gentlemen from the Sierra Leone Company and took in the view beyond the window, where snow was falling. I had taken their milky-sweet tea with them and had eaten of their dense raisin-cake. My belly was full. I felt better than I had felt for months. In fact I toyed with the idea of beating them all up, tying them together around the table and placing hot coals around the room to burn down the school and them with it. I reckon I could have done it without too much trouble. It would have been fun. But that was not our family way, and it wouldn't really help me anyway. I was already in very deep trouble, but even if the worst came to the worst and I was thrown out of the academy, I would still stand one day before my father, look him in his eye and tell him that I'd kept my first promise to him: I had not allowed a white man to beat me.

'His expulsion would cause us immense difficulties.'

'That is no concern of this academy! Are we to be governed by the demands of African politics?'

'I understand his brother is also in attendance here?'

'He is.'

'Then we may dispatch one child back to Freetown and retain the other here. No shame on either side and no scandal.'

'Robert stays with me,' I declared. 'Where I go he goes.'

All three heads turned slowly to stare at me in appalled fascination.

'Young man, did you request permission to speak?'

'Forgive me, Mr Stephen. I did not.'

'Did I or any of these gentlemen inquire as to your opinions on these matters?'

'No sir, but—!'

He silenced me with a gesture.

'Summon Mr Unwin. We shall hear what he has to say.'

A servant ushered Unwin in to stand beside the table facing me. I had given him a bloodied black eye. His nose was bandaged. He stood like a constipated vulture. Gin fumes from his breath and a tobacco-reek from his clothes quickly filled the hot room.

'This young gentleman claims you struck him in the face with your cane, Mr Unwin. Is that so?'

'That I did not do, though beat him I did.'

'How would you account for the welts on the fellow's cheeks, then?'

'Who knows what order of mischief these people may devise? The Williams boys and those in their circle have conspired to undermine me from the day they set foot in this house of learning.'

'So he, or one of his fellow pupils fabricated these wounds in order to support their allegations against you?'

'Totally unsubstantiated allegations. And the boy is a liar like all the rest.'

Reverend Venn settled back in his chair and surveyed me. 'Jupiter Williams, what have you to say for yourself? You do not deny raising your hand to your teacher?'

'No.'

'And how did you attack him?'

'Upon receiving blows to my face, sir, I punched him full-square in the belly and in the head.'

The Reverend coughed into his handerkerchief. 'Mr Unwin, can you tell us what occasioned the use of the cane on the young man?'

'Impertinence, of course,' barked the Yorkshireman. 'The boy chose to take a beating intended for his brother. I granted that wish.'

'Exactly how many strokes of the cane did you award him?'

'Six and six alone, sir. Clearly less than he deserved.'

'He has informed us that you beat him upon a mere whim, that you vowed to reduce him to slavery. That you thrashed him to the ground for no reason whatsoever, and that once defenceless and on the floor you set about his face with "relish and abandon". That you used your boots upon him. Is this true?'

Mr Unwin spluttered. I caught his eye and for the smallest part of a second I smiled especially pure demonic hatred into him, before regaining my pained, distracted contemplation of the cattle on the Common.

'Fetch the man some water. He's on the verge of collapsing.' Unwin was lowered into an armchair and a glass was soon in his hands. He did not drink it. In fact, I'm not sure I'd ever seen him drink water, or tea or milk or any cordial. We watched him gaze at the liquid for some time.

Once at ease he rose to speak with extraordinary clarity: 'Gentlemen, the choice is yours. I stand before you, a teacher of twenty years' standing. As my references attest, I have taught in some of the greatest seats of learning in this land.' Reverend Venn reached for his handkerchief. 'I have been a private tutor to the sons of our nation's finest families. I admit, I have never flinched from enforcing discipline, but have always been both firm and fair in its application. Therefore to find myself brought here, almost as a criminal, to present my case against that of a . . . a . . . a young *negro liar*, before gentlemen of my own race is, I confess, an occasion that fills me with sorrow and with shame. I have fulfilled my duties in this establishment without undue prejudice and to the best of my abilities, given the circumstances and the student body. But if the word of an African weighs more heavily in your hearts than that of your fellow Englishman, then I say, sirs, I am not suited to teach in this school and you are not worthy to govern it. Judge as you may.'

The eminent school governors asked me to leave the room.

I stood in the corridor for over half an hour, not even bothering to eavesdrop on the proceedings behind the door. I already missed the fire. I missed the tea and cakes. I missed the beautiful views beyond the window. I was ready for whatever they had to say.

A servant bade me enter.

'Jupiter Williams,' began Mr Stephen, 'it is with great regret that I am forced to inform you that the governors of the African Academy have decided that as of the spring term of this year, you may no longer be considered as part of our student body. Your violent behaviour towards your tutor, Mr Unwin, is totally unacceptable. Despite your family's honourable and long-standing ties with this country, the example that one of your rank could set back in Sierra Leone in the face of established authority is more, I fear, than the church, the nation of Great Britain or the good governance of your country could tolerate. It is with much sadness then that I will be obliged to arrange your passage back to your homeland on the next packet brig. In the meantime you will attend classes as normal and will join in school outings and enjoy all the privileges due a scholar at the African Academy.'

Mr Unwin was rubbing his hands under his chin. He half grovelled towards Mr Sharp. 'If I may be so bold as to venture one desirable outcome of this sorry tale?'

'What is that, Mr Unwin?'

'. . . That I may be afforded some assistance in the classroom whilst the lad is still under my care. After all, it would serve no purpose to have further baseless accusations flying around at this stage, would it?'

'What sort of assistance would you have in mind?'

'Well, as you can see, I have been somewhat weakened by the young gentleman's unprovoked assault and I'd be failing in my duties if I was unable to exert the necessary degree of discipline, both physical and moral, within the school which my position demands.'

'In which case, we shall arrange for you to be assisted in your duties until such time as we can arrange for the boy's departure.'

Mr Unwin coughed. 'Begging your pardon, sir, but there is someone I have in mind whom I believe might be perfect in this regard. A good fellow. A stout man. Yes, very stout.'

All the time Mr Sharp's eyes were telling me that he was very sorry for me and very, very scared about something yet to occur.

[5]

The dormitory was empty. The classroom was empty. There was no sound apart from the servants below-stairs preparing our evening meal. Then I remembered that everyone had been taken off to walk about a frozen royal park somewhere or other. I felt between the mattress and the slats of my bunk and found my favourite slingshot and a bag of missiles. It was made from intricately patterned strips of coloured leather and had been given to me by a boy of the Temne people. I had borrowed it from him when we had been comparing our slingshots for accuracy one blazing African afternoon. I tried his and he tried mine. His weapon was significantly more true in aim and made a greater impact than mine. The young African commanded me to keep it. I could do nothing to make him take it back, and he could not touch it again because he saw me kill my brother Patrick with it.

If you stand on the Common amongst the tall rushes in front of the church you would never think you were in

London. All is nature. Birdsong is the only sound. Is this the greatest city on Earth? To the west a muddy track winds towards the few houses huddled around Battersea Rise. Somewhere beyond the fields fringing the High Street is the village of Brixton and after that Camberwell. To the south are places undeserving of names. This is truly the middle of nowhere. Even the furthest outskirts of Freetown are more bustling than these silent half-villages. And to think that in three days' time I was obliged to travel far to the east of this vast bleak city with brother Robert and William Tamba to eat at the table of Sir Thomas Manton! I was not looking forward to it.

A small goose flapped out of the sky to drink by the village pond. I blew on my hands, cracked my knuckles and loaded the slingshot with a nice lead lobber. I squinted an aim halfway along its body and swung the slingshot three times at its widest arc. Even if it was a poor shot and caught the bird anywhere except the feet, the lobber would break bones and pulp muscle, leaving it incapable of flight. I loosed the lead and watched it fly straight to its target. The goose was knocked clean off its legs into the water. I wrung the bird's neck, then wrapped it in my scarf and slung it over my shoulder like a trail bag. I whistled an aimless tune to myself as I walked back to the village via the High Street.

It was quiet. Tradesmen had closed up for the day. The only activity came from the pub. It was always busy in The Goat and Ball. From our first day in Clapham we'd been instructed to avoid The Goat and Ball. It was a bad place where bad people did bad things. I peeked through the window and immediately wished I hadn't. Mr Unwin was in there. He was sharing a joke with someone. When I saw who Unwin was laughing with I knew what the joke was about. It was about me – and I was in very real trouble.

[6]

London, 18th January 1800

Dear Father,

I greet you in the name of Our Lord, Jesus Christ. I hope all is well with you and that Sierra Leone continues to prosper.

Although this is a brief note, it may well be the most difficult letter I've yet written to you.

Father, I know the confidence you have placed in me and the esteem in which our family is held. Knowing this, it is all the more painful to recount what has befallen me.

As a result of a series of incidents with the master of this academy (an uncouth fellow beneath all contempt) I regret to inform you that I have been expelled from the African Academy and, in all probability, will see you roughly a month from your reading this letter. I have no intention of abandoning Robert and he will return with me. I know our return may well signal the end of your plans for our education (especially Robert's) but I'm sure we can put our talents to good use under your instruction.

Be of good cheer and know that if I have failed you it has only been for reasons that do honour to the name of Williams.
Your loving son
Jupiter

[7]

I do not know how I managed to sleep that night. Everyone wanted to talk to me. The dormitory sounded like the lunatic asylum we were once taken to visit. How did it feel to punch Unwin in the belly? Was I beaten by the school governors? Was I going to be thrown out on to the streets of London? What would my father think?

The only person who seemed unconcerned was my brother, Robert. He was standing on a table reading aloud from the notices in the *Public Advertiser* to anyone who cared to listen. Few did.

'*Run Away From Captain Goldsmith: a middle-size negro man, having short hair and going by the name of Oliver Green, who was wearing a white jacket, a pair of black worsted breeches with stockings and a black wig. Whoever gives notice of him to Captain Richard Goldsmith of Prince's Square, Ratcliff, shall have a Guinea for a Reward.* This is the sort of country we are in!'

'It is a good country, Robert,' I corrected him. 'The best! Why do you say otherwise?'

'Yet see how our people are treated?' He flapped the newspaper in my face. 'Hunted down like dogs!'

'The fellow should have been proud to serve aboard one of His Majesty's vessels.'

'He was most likely kidnapped, Jupiter.'

'Whether kidnapped, press-ganged or a volunteer, he should have remained on board to serve his full term. That is the law. Now he's a fugitive, and to no advantage.'

'He was most likely kidnapped, Jupiter. Or a slave even. You've heard of them, haven't you?'

He turned away from me, muttering his customary 'Jupiter, stupider, Jupiter, stupider . . .' under his breath, then continued reading to William Tamba.

Why those two are friends is a mystery to me. The boy cannot understand one word in three that Robert is saying. I'm not entirely sure he knows he is in London, but he nods and smiles a lot. His stock phrase is 'Praise be to God' which he will use in every circumstance for want of better English. He pronounces this 'Press beater goat'!

And he still bores everyone to death with his story about the strange Mande-speaking black man in the bushes. He is mad. The thought of travelling with William to a strange part of this city fills me with horror. I am only going to keep an eye on Robert and our family affairs. I only hope Sir Thomas Manton's house has a good billiards table.

[8]

We knew something was wrong the moment we stepped into the classroom the following morning. Mr Unwin was smiling at us for a start. His head was tipped to one side.

'Good morning, gentlemen.' He pulled out chairs for the first few stunned pupils. 'Take your places, please.' He gave me a special greeting with a half-bow. 'Good morning, Master Williams.' His bruises made his smile ghastly. 'We have a new position for you today. Something special.' My desk had been positioned directly under the open window, to catch the worst of the frosty air. 'Pride of place, you might call it.'

Behind the desk was Bavya.

Standing at six feet and eight inches, Bavya was the tallest man in Clapham, if not the whole of South London. He was certainly the tallest man I had ever seen. He was a bare-knuckle boxer; one of a company of rough-looking men who slept above The Goat and Ball and ate and drank there as well. He was not English. Some say he came from Bohemia or Bavaria, but no one really knew. No one had ever heard him talk, although he seemed to understand all that was said to him. He loved to fight. He fought every stranger who came to The Goat and Ball. When there were no strangers to attack, he fought his friends. When his friends were absent, he would use a tree on the Common as a sparring aid. Great strips of bark had been beaten away under the onslaught of his fists. He was feared by all except Mr Unwin. He and the teacher drank together daily in silence. Once, last summer, upon hearing that Mr Unwin had been savaged by a dog belonging to Mr Simpson, the blacksmith, Bavya had calmly walked across to the forge, chosen a half-finished railing from a stack and beaten both dog and master into unconsciousness before strolling back (now using the railing as a walking stick) to finish his pot of ale and signal for another two.

It was exceedingly cold in that room. Even Mr Unwin was pacing swiftly back and forth, flapping his arms as he spoke.

'Now I hope you've all attended to the work I set you last week?'

We remembered nothing. There had been no work set whatsoever.

'The history of England from the invasion of

Julius Caesar to the Revolution of 1688. Its laws, customs, literature, arts and music. Our territories across the seas, in India, Africa, the Americas, and islands beyond number . . .'

He was talking to himself. Drunk again.

'Who can name for me our kings and queens . . .' Robert's hand was already up and Unwin moved towards it. 'The Plantagenets. In sequence.'

'Henry II, Richard I, King John, Henry III, Edward I, Edward II, Edward III, Richard II, Henry IV, Henry V, Henry VI . . .'

'Enough! You have learnt well, young Williams. Very good. Now let us see if learning runs in your family. Jupiter, stand up!'

I stood.

'Sit down!'

Bavya pressed me down into the chair.

'Stand again, Jupiter!'

I considered ignoring his command, but Bavya's railing was soon at my neck, levering me into obedience.

'And now . . . *down*!'

I sat.

'Have we any other little historians among us?'

To our astonishment, William Tamba stood up. 'I know history,' he said. 'Mande-people history.'

We (those of us who weren't Mande people – which was most of us) groaned. Mr Unwin silenced us. 'Speak, young Tamba. Shame your mockers.'

'Well,' he began. 'Mande people are the first people in Sierra Leone.' We howled in protest, but he continued. 'Many, many kings, many, many towns.'

We knew what was coming next. Usually William was as dumb as a rocking-horse, but once he started on the lineage of the Mande kings there was no stopping him. He knew all their names and relationships from generation to generation until they ended with him, of course as the future ruler of his people and the rightful ruler of all of Sierra Leone. We all gave a little sarcastic round of applause when he finished. Mr Unwin looked stunned. 'Well, who else has tales to tell? What other chroniclers do we have?'

John Thorp raised his hand and stood to tell us all about the wonderful Maroons of Jamaica and how they came to be in Sierra Leone.

I let my mind drift. I'd heard it all before many times. How those plucky, resourceful fighters had held the British at bay for over one hundred and forty years, of how they had incredible conch-shell communications from mountain to valley to mountain, of how they still retained the best African traditions, of how slavery didn't break them, but they broke slavery until they were defeated and shipped, all of them, to Sierra Leone.

For some reason Unwin was enjoying all this. He brought out a globe and an atlas and crouched down with us as we explained our various origins.

All except me, of course, I had to remain seated.

The Caulkers stood as a group to tell their unbelievable story of some crazy English pirate called Caulker from a place called Falmouth, who landed in Sierra Leone almost two hundred years ago. The English pirate liked the place and married into local royalty. He started up a string of trading posts, dealing in spices, grain, gold and people. His descendants are as black as I am, but are amongst the richest people in West Africa. Nobody likes them.

It was soon my turn to stand. I was granted permission to use the globe. I demonstrated where my father had been a slave in North America and how he had run away from his master to join the British Army. I then showed the route he and Mother took to Canada with thousands of other former slaves after the American war against the King. Then finally I traced a line from Nova Scotia across the Atlantic to Sierra Leone. The story always makes me swell with pride, but I didn't give any expression to it that day. I was too busy wondering what tricks the teacher had up his sleeve for me.

'Now Jupiter, before we continue, perhaps you can enlighten us. Why do we study history? What does it teach us?'

'History, sir, makes our own time make sense; it tells us our duties and boundaries, provides targets to reach and marks we must not overstep. The study of history is the duty of all. We must know the history of our family and friends, we must know the history of our neighbours and also that of our enemies.'

'Those are your own words?'

'They are mine.' My father had recited them to me day in and day out for over twelve years. My words.

'You do lie, child. I want to hear you speak for yourself. Plainly, this time.' He nodded to Bavya. Something very heavy, very cold and very hard indeed whipped the back of my head. I was knocked forward, but caught myself on the desk. When I turned around, I saw that Bavya hadn't used the railing. His fingers were curled lightly. He had barely tapped me with his knuckles.

I sat down slowly and unsteadily.

'So, can you answer the question, then?'

‘What question?’ In truth, I was so shocked I’d forgotten any question Unwin could have asked.

Bavya’s fist struck again. This time from above. It felt like being kicked by a horse. My head snapped backwards and I went down.

The last I remember of that day was trying to stand, and seeing that fist wobble towards me once more.

[9]

Once upon a time in Africa, I had an older brother called Patrick. We used to do everything together. We worked with our father. We were used to travelling far inland. We'd go on foot or horseback, or sometimes along the rivers. Our business was trade, exploration and the spreading of God's word. After a few years upcountry we realized we were stronger, faster, funnier, more clever and richer than anyone else we met. We were certainly more healthy and wealthy than the wretched-looking European sailors who hung around Freetown. Occasionally, ships' officers would stay with us as guests and they certainly wanted for nothing. There were more books in our house than in the rest of the country. Everybody knew us and every time we came to a new village along the river the local youth would offer challenges; skill-at-arms, memory games, wrestling, dance, storytelling.

One afternoon we had been sent ahead of Father's party on a raft to make contact with a Temne village by a waterfall near Charlotte village. Father often sent us before him. He was convinced that two unarmed young men would get a better welcome than a host of twenty armed strangers.

I can't recall the place or the customs very well, but the young men of the village wasted no time at all in demonstrating their prowess with native slingshots. They were good. Birds were picked off in flight.

We could not resist showing off our own slingshots and special care was taken to demonstrate our lead lobs, which we doubted they had ever seen before.

A final test was called for. Small brass and wood shields were passed to us and we were invited to stand still twenty-five paces away from their best marksmen. We were expected to deflect all incoming missiles.

That task was fairly easy and we quickly grew bored of it. Patrick demanded that the positions be reversed. We would throw. They would parry. Needless to say they were utterly humiliated and many of them walked away with swellings and cracked bones to remember us by.

They were in awe of us by the end of that afternoon and demanded a final display of our powers. The distance would be doubled and Patrick and I would be pitted against each other. One youth gave me his slingshot as a mark of respect and begged me to use it.

It was an excellent weapon but Patrick still managed to dance through its volleys. The entire community seemed to have turned out to watch the tournament. If we managed to enthral them sufficiently we would be their heroes. They would not just want our friendship and advice, but also our father's business, his textiles, his spices, his timber, his contacts, all the business and all the religion.

Patrick was playing fancy now; jumping from crouches to swat away my first barrage of rocks. Then he started playing clever by angling the shield against the sun to blind me or using it like a bat to knock the missiles back towards me. The crowd loved him. People always did. He always had some new trick up his sleeve.

When he started tipping my rocks over into the waterfall behind him with mere shrugs, I decided that I'd had enough. He was making me look foolish and needed to be taught a lesson.

I loaded the slingshot with two stones instead of one and kept a third in my hand in reserve. The villagers were mocking me directly now, mimicking my frustration, so I abandoned any idea of caution. I slung the rocks, one after the other in rapid succession.

There was nothing he could have done to protect himself. The first he batted away, the second caught the inside of his shield as he brought it down to ward off the sun's glare. The third slammed into his face and knocked him sideways. He staggered backwards.

The last I saw of him was his heels as he fell into the water. He was sucked into the rapids and flushed over the waterfall. I didn't dive after him but I should have. I was a stronger swimmer. I could have saved his life. Instead I killed him.

I still talk to him – every day. I talk to him a lot, mostly when I'm scared and don't know what to do. Patrick always knew the right thing and the right way to do it. I talk to him especially when I'm sick. I'm not often ill, but I was in the sick ward for a few days recovering from the beating Bavya had given me. Talking to Patrick gave me strength. I needed it.

The pain wasn't the real problem. My muscles were hurting and I felt rough from my face to my feet. The real problem was the sick ward. They should have called it the death ward. No one ever left it alive. Too many of our young men entered that room with measles and colds and shaking flu and expired there.

I wasn't alone in the sick ward. Another boy was shivering and sweating in a neighbouring bed. He was wild-eyed. Enormous bubbles of saliva burst from his mouth. He did not, or could not speak. I turned my back on him in terror and fell back to sleep. When I turned to face his bed again he was gone. I couldn't even remember his name. I knew we'd been introduced at some stage and his face was familiar, but I never remember names.

The next thing I knew, Bavya was at my side wiping my face with a damp rag. A look of tenderness crossed his eyes and I wondered if he had children of his own somewhere. Unwin peered from behind his shoulder, as if afraid I might strike him from my bed of pain. He was right to be afraid.

'See – you see how we tend and care for you, wretch though you are. This is still a Christian house!'

Christian indeed. I pictured him in hell, being turned on a spit by cackling, skipping demons.

'Your brother instructed me to send you his farewell.'

'His farewell?'

'Yes, his farewell.'

'What do you mean?' I struggled to my elbows.

'He is gone,' Unwin flapped his fingers, 'gone with the Tamba child. Away on whatever business takes you people into that city.'

'Where is he? Where is Robert?' I tried to raise myself and failed.

'He is far away – east, beyond St George's in the east.' He was speaking in riddles.

Bavya laughed long and loud, then bent his head and spoke to me for the first time. Three words. 'Robert. Au. Revoir.' He laughed again and waved a baby bye-bye.

My head started to spin. Robert was gone. Out there in the largest city in the world with a gurgling imbecile for company and guidance. I looked at the sky beyond the window and gauged the quality of the light.

'What day is it?' I pushed my feet off the bed away from Bavya and tried to slide on to the floor. The agony that shot through my legs was beyond description. I crumpled to the floor. 'What day is it?'

'Bavya,' Unwin commanded, 'lift the boy and lay him down that he may heal. I will let the maids know that he's ready for some pea soup. He will be strong soon enough. I've work for this one, aye! Work aplenty for him.'

Bavya lifted and dropped me on to the bed like a shilling's worth of flour. The pair of them chuckled darkly as they left the room.

Have you ever tasted green? Have you ever chewed a stalk of grass, I mean? That is to say, really chewed it, then sucked it till the green is gone? Then you spit the clump of fibres and see they are paler than straw? That taste. Pure green. I know it well.

Once upon a time in Africa, Patrick, Father and I made an extremely long and dangerous trip upriver. With fourteen helpers we poled and hauled three rafts full of samples and Bibles along a river banked with jungle. Everything was green: green water, green land and even once a green sky full of green birds.

We got lost in the bends of some unknown waterways and soon we started to run out of food. Our helpers ran away. We had been abandoned two hundred miles away from home. The guides had even taken the last of our cornmeal and dried fish. We walked through the jungle. We became very hungry very soon. When we couldn't trap any bush-pigs or snakes, we ate sweet-nut leaves and took water from vomit-inducing green streams.

But we knew we'd survive. We were tough. We were the Williams family and there was not a single moment in which we thought we'd perish.

Of course we made it back to Freetown. In fact, I always think of that week of hunger and madness with Father and Patrick as one of the happiest times of my life.

* * *

Mary was spooning pea soup into my mouth. It tasted wonderfully green. Mary was a moon-faced maid who worked in all parts of the school, and she had been serving black people long enough to know how to salt food judiciously. She hadn't only brought soup. There were slices of juicy pork secreted under a towel as well, which she slipped into the dish once Bavya was out of the way.

As she sat and spooned she was joined by a new girl whose name I didn't know, but she stank of cheese.

'When's he coming back?' I asked her. She knew I knew she was overly fond of Robert. Everybody except the teaching staff knew that.

'He should have been back yesterday, Master Jupiter.' She could not look at me directly.

'Yesterday!' I sat straight up in the bed in a single movement. Blood pounded at my temples.

'Yesterday! What day is it today, girl?'

'It is the Lord's day, sir. It is a Sunday.'

'Then my little brother is truly gone. He is lost.'

'Or taken away,' whispered Mary. Her cheesy friend nodded to herself.

As if she knew something whereof she could not speak.

[10]

I had always looked after Robert.

Since arriving in England my little brother had not been out of my sight for more than five minutes. I was not overly fond of the little fellow though he was sometimes very funny (as long as I was not the butt of his jokes). He often annoyed me with his know-it-all ways, and he loved more than anything to demonstrate the scope and depth of his learning. But he thought reading was everything. It was not. There were worlds upon worlds beyond the pages of his books. Worlds of terror, pain and loss that I knew well. It was my sacred duty to protect him from these realities until he was old enough to face them himself. I had failed.

Unwin had work for me, to be sure. He called it hard work. Shameful work. Women's work. For Mr William Unwin, the worst fate that could befall a young man of means and position was to be ordered to do women's work: washing, cooking and cleaning – amongst women. He thought he could break me by putting me to work in the kitchen and the laundry. He was wrong.

Unlike him, I liked the company of women and I enjoyed squeezing around them as we laboured in the steam of the kitchen or sweated over tubs of laundry. Being amongst those plain, hearty women helped to take my mind away from Robert's absence. After a couple of afternoons engaged in these activities, I was slowly coming back to life. And as my strength increased, so did my fears for my brother – and for myself. I could never have imagined it was possible for any human being to feel so lonely as I did then.

I was in a terrible situation. Unwin made sure I was kept out of contact with the rest of the boys at the academy. Not that any of them would ever seek to contact me. I had never sought popularity and there was not one amongst them I could call a friend. But I needed to find out what had become of Robert and William Tamba. Reluctantly, I turned to Mary.

Now Mary is a nice girl. She is a good girl, but she is in love with my brother Robert and has been, by all accounts, since his arrival in Clapham. This is something I have tried to ignore for a very long time, and it must be said that she is a very unsuitable consort for Robert. I do not object on any grounds of her complexion (her skin is as fair as may be expected of any daughter of these islands) – after all there is no

Biblical teaching against unions between the different branches of the family of man. No, I am concerned about Mary because she is a member of the serving classes and, even though our grandparents were slaves, in this age we, the Williams family, were born to lead by example, and she has none to set.

On my second morning of freedom from the sick ward, she came to me as I was peeling potatoes.

'He heard them talking, Master Jupiter. He heard them.'

Now having been around the sun fourteen times, I am well accustomed to the ways of those who start and develop conversations with you as though you can read their minds. I continued peeling as if nothing was unusual, which of course, it was not. 'Who heard who talking about what, Mary?'

'Me uncle, dahn the pahb, heard Mr Unwin talking to Mr Bavya. Talking about Robert and Billy Tamba.'

Her uncle was Mr Simpson, the blacksmith. Like many young women who could not read, the chatter reported from pubs formed her entire frame of reference. I nodded to her as if I understood and was totally sympathetic to what she was trying to say. Then she said: 'They've been taken.'

I stopped peeling.

'Robert and Billy Tamba, they've been taken. Me uncle's been talking about it. Everyone's talking about it. The school doesn't know what's going on, but we do. We've heard. It was highwaymen, they say. Took them on the Mile End road. They never even made it to Stratford, looks like. You're going to look for him, aintcha?'

'No, I'm going to find him, Mary, and I'll need your help.'

She smiled.

[11]

I moved quickly.

Father had fitted our luggage with secret compartments. He had made sure we had enough money for emergencies: fifteen pounds each. I put on a double layer of clothing to protect against the cold. I scanned the list of Father's London contacts. One immediately caught my eye. The Reverend Henry Wilde (one of his oldest friends, apparently) lived in Bethnal Green, east London. Stratford was also in the east. All I had to do was get there.

Mary found me as I was stealing cold meats, cheese and a small loaf to take on my journey.

'Me uncle will help you.'

I uncorked a bottle of cordial and took a swig. 'Mr Simpson, God bless him!'

'Well, he's no friend of Mr Unwin and his dog-beating mate. He'll help you get away. He's waiting for you at the forge. Go now. There's no one about. Get away while you can, Jupiter!'

As quickly and quietly as possible, I made my way to the side door. Seemingly from nowhere, the corridor was suddenly full of boys. Somehow word had got out that I would attempt to run away.

The Caulkers presented me with my slingshot, which I'd forgotten in my hurry. Other boys appeared and offered boiled sweets, a pocket Bible, paper and ink, odd coins, and a half pie. If I could get across the yard, throw the bag over the wall and pull myself after it, I could be safely inside the forge in under one minute.

Sleet, or maybe hail (I can never distinguish between the varieties of misery English weather offers) was falling and I fastened a scarf about my neck. I eased open the door and snuck out, keeping to the side of the building. As I turned the final corner I felt myself being tugged backwards by the neck. Bavya was pulling on my scarf and Unwin was with him. I have no idea where they came from or how they managed to move so silently, but I knew they weren't there to offer fruit and flowers for my journey.

'We've a task for ye, Jupiter, lad. It's the weather vane, you see. Somewhat askew in this foul weather it has become. Most unstable. Needs straightening and you're just the fellow to do it. Come now.'

One-handedly, Bavya lifted me off the ground by the neck and carried me.

'Have you no tools for me?'

'Tools? You will use your bare hands!' Mr Unwin gestured using his own. 'Now climb!'

Bavya clapped in front of my face. It sounded like a gunshot.

I would not say I have a fear of heights and I would not say I am afraid of ice, but when the two are put together I am terrified. Every time I have been on an icy ledge, roof or mountainside something bad has happened. Not necessarily to me, but to someone else. During our first winter in London, two boys from the academy had to be fished out from a frozen lake after they fell through the ice. They very nearly died. Stephen Caulker was one of them. I was the other.

I couldn't let my tormentors see my fear.

The ladder was old and rungs were missing. This was no problem for me as it was the ladder we all used throughout the summer when we used to escape on to the roof to smoke our pipes. That is, until William Tamba had a coughing fit and slid off into the horse trough. But ascending the ladder was second nature to me.

I like to imagine I impressed them. I grabbed a

stretch of guttering and rocked it to test its strength. It wasn't too bad. I swung my foot up and balanced half my weight on it whilst looking out for a handhold. There was nowhere to grip, just smooth, icy slates, one after another to seeming infinity. I reckoned that I could ease myself along the guttering if I flattened my body against the roof.

As I shifted position I made the mistake of looking down. My tormentors were grinning. Bavya brandished his railing as a reminder of what awaited me should I descend.

Little by little, I edged across the base of the roof until I came to a line of clay markers. I had climbed these before and knew they would hold firm. Hooking my fingers under their upper edges, I climbed up to the weather vane. It spun wildly in the wind. I straddled the roof. I was freezing and wondering what to do next when a very deep voice called from some way away.

'What on Earth is that child doing up there in this weather!'

It was Mr Thornton, one of the school's patrons.

'What is the meaning of this? Summon that young African immediately!'

Mr Thornton was probably the richest man in Clapham. He was a banker of some sort and everyone behaved as if they lived in constant fear of him. He was also an acquaintance of my father. They had some business together, of which I knew nothing. Indeed, when he found out that we would be attending the academy he had insisted that we stay with him in his mansion rather than the school's dormitory. Father instructed us to decline the offer and to eat and sleep under the same conditions as the rest of our brethren lest we appear stand-offish. As a result, Robert and I have kept our distance from him and diverted his attempts at familiarity into more neutral discussion. But at that moment up on the roof, his pompous tones sounded as though an angel had been sent from heaven to guide me to safety. I started on my way down immediately.

I overheard Unwin concocting some story about how I was seeking to avoid punishment by taking refuge on the roof. They were explaining how it was apparently in the nature of our people to seek shelter out of reach in high places. He was certainly an original thinker, I'll give him that.

Thornton seemed unconvinced. He was leaning out of a very extravagant-looking carriage. His face, where it wasn't wrapped up in scarves and collars, was red.

'I know this boy!' he declared. 'Jupiter Williams.

How are you, my young fellow? Get down from there immediately!'

I picked up my sack and strolled over to him as if we were old acquaintances.

'Mr Thornton, how pleasant it is to meet you once again.'

I took the liberty of opening the door to his carriage. He waved me in without a word to either of the men connected with the school.

'My father wrote to instruct me that I should convey his best wishes to you and your family, sir. I understand he was quite anxious to receive correspondence from you.'

'Was he indeed? What else did he say?'

'I cannot exactly recall, Mr Thornton. The post between here and my home country is far from regular. My last letter from him was some time ago. My memory fails me.'

'Nonetheless, you must consider yourself my guest, for a few hours, at least.' He looked over my shoulder. 'You have a younger brother, have you not? I trust he will be joining us?'

'I'm afraid you'll have to ask my teacher, Mr Unwin,' I declared in a purposefully loud voice. 'He will have a far better idea as to his whereabouts at this time than I.

Is that not so, sir?' I turned to fix the schoolmaster with a stare of absolute contempt before getting into the banker's vehicle.

Unwin stared at the hard icy ground. Bavya met my eyes, matching my level of hatred with his own. He held the railing in his fist like a dagger.

Mr Thornton made sure I was settled into my seat before waving twice: once to his coachman and secondly at the school buildings, which quickly vanished behind us.

12

Mr Thornton lived in an enormous property on the other side of the common. He showed me around parts of the house. I recognized a lot of the things he was showing me and I pretended to be impressed. It was what Father called 'typical rich Englishman's stuff'; unread, ready-made, batch-bought libraries full of books in Greek, Latin, French and sometimes English. There was lots of Sevres porcelain, poorly-made imitation Chinese screens and vases, copies of paintings by deservedly lesser-known Italian and Dutch painters. It was the sort of 'stuff' we had at home, but this was all of much better quality. Mr Thornton must have been incredibly rich.

He seemed to have more servants working for him than worked at the academy. I stopped counting after twenty-two.

'Are you thirsty, boy?'

'I am, sir.'

He ordered a butler to tell a cook to command a footman to instruct a young black boy to bring me a glass of gooseberry cordial. The boy was wearing a turban. Mr Thornton noticed me staring at him. 'Francis is no slave, Jupiter. He is free to come and go as he pleases. He is his own man.'

I had never seen the boy around the village before. Perhaps he never left the house. He probably didn't need to. He seemed well fed and happy enough. He was about the same age as Robert.

'He can read and write, can't you, Francis?'

The boy nodded.

'All servants in this house receive instruction in the basics of civilized life. Why, even the garden-boys – Horace!' He called for one of them.

I recognised the garden-boy as a local man. He was over fifty years old.

'Horace here has been schooled in scripture and, of course, so has Francis. Horace!' Mr Thornton swivelled to face the gardener, who looked as if he was about to cry. 'Horace, the Book of Amos is followed by which book?'

The poor man looked bewildered. He caught my eye and I mouthed the word 'Obadiah' to him behind his master's back.

'And after Obadiah, Francis?'

'Jonah!' snapped the little houseboy.

'Horace, what's next? Quickly now, quickly!'

'Micah,' he muttered, having managed to read my lips.

'Nahum!' screamed the young wretch.

'Very good, Francis.' The banker patted his head for longer than was necessary. I hate it when white people do that. 'Horace?'

'Babbacuckoo? Rubba-bucka? Cook-a-book? Oh, I don't know, sir!'

'Habakkuk, man! Habakkuk!' Thornton looked like he was about to strike Horace, and I believe he would have done had I not been there. 'Complete the list, Francis.'

'Zephaniah, Haggai, Zechariah and Malachi.'

While Thornton was busy praising the youth, Horace mimed induced vomiting. I tried not to laugh.

'Francis, will you be so kind as to escort our guest to the door. I'm sure his teachers will be wondering where he is.'

I thanked the rich man for his time and promised to report to him regularly on the welfare of the boys at the school.

Not a single word passed between Francis and I as we made our way through that vast house, though I could see he seemed eager to make my acquaintance.

At the door he offered me his hand.

I don't know why I clouted him, but I did. Twice. I know it hurt him because it certainly made my hand sting. His head was harder than coconut.

As I opened the gate to the Common, I looked back. He was still standing there staring at me. Rage and confusion swirled in his swelling face.

I saluted him mockingly and went to Mr Simpson, the blacksmith.

[13]

I walked easily through the backstreets off the High Street safe in the knowledge that the school would not dare interfere with any business between me and Mr Thornton. At least not until ten o'clock.

Mercifully, the blacksmith's forge was still open. Its strong, hot, red light beckoned me. The clang of Mr Simpson's hammer working metal on his anvil comforted me greatly and, for a moment, reminded me of Freetown and the hours Robert and I passed studying ironworkers there. Robert knew all about iron; where and how it was mined and how it was refined. For a moment I felt as if he was walking to the blacksmith's with me, filling my ears with obscure facts and figures about the history of steel production. I choked back a sob at the thought that I might never see him again.

I knocked at the half-open door. There was no reply so I shouldered my way in and shouted hello from just over the threshold.

The metalworker looked up, shrugged, and flicked

his face at a clock on a work surface. 'She said you'd be here over an hour ago.'

'I'm sorry,' I began, 'I have been delayed.'

'I don't like waiting,' he continued.

I said I was sorry.

'I've been a-waiting some time now.'

I said I was sorry again.

'Time is money for a man such as myself, and I've been a-waiting and a-waiting for you, young man.'

'Please forgive my imposition, Mr Simpson.' I reached for my purse. 'I believe you know the reason for my approaching you in this irregular manner.'

The blacksmith held his hand out to me. 'I'm not wanting your money, young sir. Assisting you and your brother is the least I can do to get my own back on that pair of rogues!'

I shook his hand.

I had never shaken the hand of a white adult in friendship before. It felt both totally right and totally wrong.

'Mary said your young fella was in trouble. It's the talk of the village. We all know what's going on. All of us except them churchical types what live about the Common.'

'I hear tell it was highwaymen,' I said, 'that

Robert was kidnapped and taken, perhaps for sale.' Just voicing those words almost caused me to collapse, so I gripped the back of a chair and leant forward as I spoke, masking my fear with a determined posture.

'No p'raps about it. Money is money, and there's them as buys and sells the likes of you. If I wasn't an ironworking man, who's to say I wouldn't be doing the same thing meself – in fact a cousin of mine what lives over Bristol way, 'e was known to dabble somewhat in the Jamaickee trades. Did all right for 'isself. Better than me an' Mary's papa, that's for sure. Now, if I had my time again, who's to say—'

'My good man, I need a horse!' I shouted to distract him from that line of unsavoury speculation.

He laughed in my face. Loudly. 'An 'orse! You? You? An 'orse!' He laughed again. Deafeningly this time. 'When's the last time you've seen a black boy on an 'orse? On 'is own? Jus' gallopin' along? Naahh! I can't give you one of my good animals. Don't care 'ow much money you've got. You'll never make it over the river. Never make it past Bermondsey before you're brought back kicking an' screaming.'

I disliked this man's tone. We were all gentlemen at the academy and as such I was entitled to a steed that suited my station in life. I feared he was trying to sell me a nag. But I was wrong.

'There's another way for you to leave the village.'

I was all ears.

'You know the wharf at Battersea?'

I did. It was where we went for our boatbuilding lessons.

'Well, I've a delivery to make this evening. The bargeman's a friend of mine. He'll look after you. Perhaps you'd be so kind as to see my cargo makes it all the way down the river in one piece? He's a very shrewd man, Mr Picton . . .'

[14]

I travelled to the river hidden in a wagon full of loose wrought-iron bedframes, railings, grates and other hard, knobbly or pointed things which threatened to blind or neuter me.

Mr Simpson would not take any money for his kindness, but instead pushed me on to the vessel, saying: 'I've told him you're a servant to Mr Stephen and that you're being sent downriver to sing for a friend of his.'

'Sing!' I am a very poor liar and an even worse singer. 'Why did you tell him that?'

'I had to tell him something, and the truth isn't going to help you on your way out of here, is it? Besides, I hear you boys sing every Sunday in church. You've marvellous voices, all of you.'

He had obviously never heard me and William Tamba perform a duet.

'I am certain you could still tell him the truth. He must help me. He is one of my race.'

'He is, young man, but Mr Picton is also a

gentleman. An English gentleman. He's not a law-breaker, you'll see.' He shook my hand again. 'Go with God, Jupiter.'

At no point had I given him my name.

A little cabin had been built in the middle of the deck. A crewman pushed me through it. 'E's in there,' he said.

Mr Picton was very fat indeed. The armchair he sat on was invisible. I looked from him to the door I had just walked through and back again. There was no way he could have entered the room using that entrance, even if he squeezed himself sideways. There was an open skylight in the ceiling to air the hot room, and I tried to imagine him being lowered through it. Or maybe the cabin had been built around him and he never left it.

He ate a leg of lamb as he looked me up and down. 'Very fine clothes you're wearing. Who's your master's tailor?'

'Schweitzer and Davidson of Cork Street,' I blurted without thinking.

Mr Picton nearly choked on his food. 'Wha . . . ! Upon my word. Such extravagance lavished on servants! You have a very good master, I see.'

I nodded.

'How are you called?'

'Jupiter, sir.'

'Jupiter? Jupiter – by Jove!' He laughed and laughed and laughed at his little joke, and I laughed along with him as if I hadn't heard it one hundred times before.

'You understood my joke?'

'Why, yes, sir. Jupiter was the King of the Roman gods and Jove is how he is known in English.'

He stared at me. A strip of lamb hung from the corner of his mouth. 'How do you know these things? Your master has given you an education?'

'He has.'

He shook his head. 'My master, Mr Phillips, was also a very good soul. Like a son to him, I was. He made me the man I am today. From slave to this – not bad, eh?' He looked about the tiny cabin as if he was a duke surveying his estates. 'She's a fine-looking ship, isn't she?'

'She is very nice, Mr Picton. You must have worked very hard.' There was no way I could tell him that his barge would have made a very poor show against the fleets of river and coastal vessels that some families from the academy owned and operated in Sierra Leone.

I begged to take my leave from him in order to relieve myself.

'Over the side,' he said, waving his leg of lamb.

As I stood on deck peeing into the Thames I realized just how much I missed being on the water. Father's ships carried cattle, grain, spices, and often more than five tonnes of rice upriver at a time. Boatbuilding was taught at the school and it was my favourite subject. My notebooks and sketchbooks were full of boats and ships of all kinds. Besides, the world looked better from a gently rocking deck. The Thames crinkled around the prow where the current ran faster. For a moment all seemed well with the world.

We were making our way with impressive speed and skill. The water was full of every kind of ship imaginable, from navy frigates to rowboats, and all jostled for space. The lights of London sparkled in the river and lit up the faces of the crew. They were all white. I couldn't deny Picton his success as a businessman but surely he could have found even one black hand to man his vessel.

'Boy! Jupiter, boy! When you're done with your watering, come back in here!'

Reluctantly, I obeyed.

'Sing me a song!' he commanded.

'I beg your pardon, sir?'

'Sing me a song. C'mon, boy. I demand it. Payment for your passage.'

He sang his way up and down a few scales. His voice was a strangely immaculate contralto – clear, fluid and beautiful. For the next half-minute it floated perfectly through fragments of Mozart, Cherubini and other pieces whose composers were unknown to me. He paused, sighing heavily. 'Singing was always my first love. Like you, it was my master who introduced me to great music. Let us sing now. Together!'

I froze. He cleared his throat. I cleared mine. He hit a note I recognized as high C and motioned me to do the same. The note I produced was close to C but it was far from high. Mr Picton eyed me with great curiosity before producing a mellow bellowing sound which he invited me to join him in.

Have you ever heard the noise a cow makes just before it is about to be slaughtered? The poor beast knows it is about to be murdered and knows there is nothing whatsoever it can do about it. The sound I made was something like that and it wasn't musical at all.

The businessman raised himself from his seat. His mass took up almost two-thirds of the room. He edged across the space with surprising speed and was soon between me and the door.

'Sing for me, Jupiter. Sing for me.'

I dared not attempt anything technical, sophisticated or even formal, so I sang a song I had learnt from English sailors in Freetown.

Come cheer up, my lads! 'Tis to glory we steer,
To add something more to this wonderful year;
To honour we call you, not press you like slaves,
For who are so free as the sons of the waves?

Heart of oak are our ships, heart of oak are our men;
We always are ready, steady, boys, steady!
We'll fight and we'll conquer again and again.

We ne'er see our foes but we wish them to stay,
They never see us but they—

'You are no singer! Who are you? *What* are you?'

'My name is Jupiter Williams, Mr Picton. I am searching for my brother who I believe has been kidnapped.'

'Kidnapped, you say? So, he's a runaway like yourself?'

'I am no runaway, sir.'

'You have no master?'

'I am free-born and was a student at the African Academy.'

His frown proved that he had never heard of the place. Good.

'Jupiter, you have shown yourself to be a liar, and I have found to my cost that a liar is very often also a thief. I will keep you on board my ship until we dock and the correct authorities can establish your true identity.'

He opened the door a fraction and called for help. Before the cry had left his lips I was up on the table and jumping for the skylight. In my panic, I slipped on his meal of greasy meat and skidded painfully to the floor. I had forgotten how fast he could move, and he was soon grinning above me and cracking his fingers in anticipation of the punishment he would administer.

Seized by terror, I sprang bodily from the floor back on to the table and, in a single motion, leapt up towards the skylight. My little sack was still against the small of my back and I was squeezing myself through the square when I felt a big fat hand around my left foot. Then two. Cesar Picton was pulling me back into the room. I managed to kick his hands away, but he caught my foot a second time and adjusted his hold. Now he had a firmer grip. It was growing tighter. Tight enough to squeeze off my shoe. And at that I panicked. Regardless of what else happened to me, I wouldn't be shoeless in this world. I released my grip on the skylight and dropped knee-first into his face. He did not get up.

Our scuffle had attracted the others on board, and I heard their cries of 'Are you all right, Mr Picton?' from beyond the door. Clearly they were too terrified of either their master or myself to enter the room unbidden. Peeking through a crack in the door, I noticed a couple of the men were carrying nasty-looking hand tools. Using my fat, unconscious host's belly as a trampoline, I bounced cleanly up through the skylight, took my bearings, and dived overboard into the murky Thames.

The water was so cold that I gasped from shock. Unfortunately, I was still underwater, kicking for the surface, when that occurred. A draught of icy, muddy liquid got sucked into my stomach and I began to panic. My fear was so great I could barely move. And when my head finally broke the water my shrieks must have been heard all the way to Kent.

It was less than thirty strokes to the riverbank, but that was the longest, coldest, filthiest and most painful swim of my entire life. My muscles were spasming crazily and knotting as I nodded my way to safety. After a while I was not really swimming, but pulling myself through the water as if on an invisible rope. I was so stiff when I made the shore that I could not stand, or even crouch into a crawl. I rolled myself towards an upturned rowing boat and, like a snake, wriggled underneath it.

The boat was no use whatsoever as a windbreak. In fact it worsened my plight. Because it could not rest flush with the rocky ground, it served only to channel the stronger currents of frosty air into my shelter. I needed to get comfortable, but my legs and arms were numb. I curled up.

Sleep came immediately, and it brought a delicious warmth: the warmth of Africa. It felt so good. I dreamt I was walking through Freetown, towards the Cotton Tree. People were saying hello to me in happy, soothing voices. People were walking with me. I could hardly remember what my mother looked like, but I knew she was the kind lady with the parasol. Father was there too. I was surprised to see him there, just strolling idly through the day. He was always so busy. Even as he walked and talked with us, he kept dipping into a book. We were walking for a very long time, never seeming to get any nearer to the Cotton Tree.

'Is Robert not coming with us today, Mama?'

'Your brother is not yet here.' Her whisper sounded

very loud. Like a hiss, in fact. 'He is not yet here.'

I turned to my father. He was reading his book and shaking his head. 'Why didn't you tell us, Jupiter?' he asked.

'What should I have told you, Father?'

'About your brother, my son.'

'But hasn't Mama said, he is not here?' Indeed she was still repeating it, and I dearly wished for her to stop.

'No, Jupiter. I speak of your *other* brother, Patrick. Why did you not tell us? You never told us what really happened. I was so looking forward to seeing him here. But he is not here. He is not here! He is not here!'

They were both chanting it now. I was so very afraid. The sun sank with great speed as they repeated those dreadful words. The sky turned suddenly black. All light and heat drained from the scene. I felt myself running into infinite darkness. The voices of my parents kept pace with me. They were screaming my name now. Screaming with every kind of feeling a parent could have. I tried to outrun them: zigzagging from nowhere to nowhere.

Then I was rising, being pulled up beyond the call of the voices. I was yanked upwards so fast I began to scream. My ascent ended with a loud *crack* and I woke up to find myself sitting upright, having banged my head on a seat of the upturned boat.

I was in the grip of a mixture of absolute agony and utter boredom. It was clear I was very close to freezing to death. I had to move now. I rolled out, raised myself, and began to hop madly like the kangaroo I once saw at a fair.

After a while I started to feel my blood moving again. I was enjoying the feeling so much that I didn't notice the two layabouts wearing red scarves at the foot of the river stairs. They were laughing at me and mimicking my movements. They stopped their mockery when I lurched crab-like towards them with bunched fists. I said 'Boo!' to them and they meekly stepped aside to let me use the stairs.

'Are you with the Blackgang, then?' called one of them.

'Nah, leave it, Jack. Leave it,' said the other.

I continued up into the town without looking over my shoulder.

15

I straightened my damp clothes as well as I could and, attempting my best impression of an educated young gentleman going about his lawful business, I hobbled off in search of food and fire.

I was soon well and truly lost amongst the narrowest, noisiest streets imaginable. Though night had fallen, a market was still crowded. Lanterns and candles were everywhere and, had it not been for the distinctly low order of person native to these parts, I would have thought myself in fairyland.

But it was not the English faces that caught my eye. I had never seen so many black people before anywhere in London. I looked into every face, young and old, as if they would hold news of my brother, as if he had been this way and left signs of his passing in the frowns and scowls which greeted me.

Some of these people were surely slaves. Father had told us that the English were the world's greatest traders in human lives.

And there were others of my race here brushing

arrogantly through the crowds, meeting the gaze of all who passed. More strangeness. There were young black people here who, apart from their faces, dressed, talked and behaved exactly like their white English friends. Or did that make them black English people? I was confused.

But I was also excited. Dotted around these streets were also people I recognized only from pictures and descriptions in geography lessons: Chinamen, Turks, Hindus and dozens of others too bizarre in dress or manner to classify.

I was fascinated by the babble of different languages, and was so keenly listening to the music of all these voices in one space that I almost missed a most wondrous sight: the Tower of London. There was no mistaking it. Those rounded base walls and four towers with pennants flying were known to every child. My heart soared to see it. And how strange that such a sight should stand hardly a stone's throw away from one of the roughest parishes in London.

My astonishment grew. Here was the largest city on Earth and the capital of its most powerful nation, and yet rich and poor, black and white, were jumbled amongst one another seemingly at random. It made no sense to me, yet I liked it, even though it stank of rotten fish and every second face sweated doom and exuded menace.

I liked it!

I went into the first public house I could find. It was a low, smoky set of rooms. Half a dozen drinkers leant about the place making small talk. Whilst no one appeared to comment on my presence amongst them, I sensed that their small talk suddenly got much smaller.

The landlord, a man almost as broad as his bar, asked: 'And how may I serve our . . . young . . . *black* . . . gentleman?'

I warmed to the fellow immediately and ordered a barley water.

The small talk became minuscule.

'We drink strong ale, spirits and fortified wines here, my friend. What will you have?'

One person coughed.

'Erm, a pint of your finest ale please, landlord!' I had always wanted to say that, even though I have always loathed beer of any kind with a passion. 'And is your kitchen open, my good man?'

'It is. What you 'avin'? We've got fried herring and potatoes, fried herring and potatoes, or fried herring. And potatoes.'

'Ah, I think I'll have the fried herring and potatoes, please.'

The fireplace was roaring, gorgeous and inviting. I took my ale from the counter and sat down.

'Oi you! Money!'

I edged back to the counter and untwisted a big, soggy pound note from my purse.

Mr Unwin once assured us that there were life forms so small as to be invisible to the human eye yet visible under microscopic lenses. Should such creatures be capable of conversation, I have no doubt that the noise of it would roar above that silence which descended about me on production of paper money in that low house.

'Ooo, I say now!' the landlord seemed to wink at an audience. 'I'll just get some change for our . . . young . . . *black* . . . gentleman. Won't be a minute, now.'

I never saw him again. But after a while, on my own by the fire, a dish of fried herring and onions and potatoes appeared which I ate with great relish. My pint of ale wasn't too bad either. I drank it all.

I had never been in a public house on my own before. It was not too bad a place. Wood smoke and tobacco fumes shrouded all in an agreeably warm gloom. The murmured conversations sounded soothing enough. My clothes were drying nicely, my belly was full of good, greasy food and fresh, corny ale. The beer had almost blunted my fear of never seeing Robert again and, had it not been for the thieving landlord, I would have considered ordering another drink.

Making sure I was not followed from the pub, I set off towards Bethnal Green. After an hour, when the Tower of London came into view again, I realized I had walked in a circle. I had not seen one single face I trusted on sight. All, African and otherwise, looked like villains. A couple of very unclean-looking girls of my own age had tried to entice me into a cellar to 'get to know me' because I had 'a nice face'. I had to use light force to free myself from their clutches. Another time I had to run in fear of my life from some drunkard with a strange jarring accent, who came after me with a cutlass, screaming to the heavens that he would skin my black hide and tear my guts out. I could look after myself well enough, but I was extremely tired and my mind was growing dull. I had no wish to walk these streets all night. I needed to consider my choices. I found a sheltered alley, sat down and promptly fell asleep.

I woke to find a hand on my shoulder.

'My friend.' The voice was measured and warm. 'My young friend, are you in trouble?'

The speaker was a plainly-dressed man of my rank. I stood to face him.

'I am in no trouble, good sir. Merely tired from the day's exertions.'

'Is it your master, boy? Does he beat you? Have you run away? Perhaps I can help. Our congregation often assists—'

'I am a free man, sir, and master of myself! My business is my own, but perhaps you can help me.'

He seemed surprised, even disappointed, that I spoke English so well, or that I was capable of speech at all.

'Free, you say? And yet you appear lost to the world . . .'

Remembering my experience with Picton, I bit my tongue. 'I mean, sir, that I am free to come and go as I please. My master is a generous man. A man of the church. I was sent on an errand and have quite lost my way.'

'Which church would that be? I know them all.'

'It is the church of St Matthew, Bethnal Green. My master is the Reverend Wilde.'

'Bethnal Green! Why that is some distance from

here. Would I be wrong in supposing that a young man such as yourself can read?'

'You would not be wrong, sir.'

'Then I shall draw you a map.' He took a pencil stub and sketched the route on a tear of brown paper.

I ran all the way.

16

It was a tiny house. A tiny woman answered the door. The sight of a black face at the porch caused her to faint. The man who stepped over her to greet me had a monkey on his shoulder.

'Why bless my soul, Patrick, bless my soul!'

'Erm, Reverend Wilde—!'

'Come in, Patrick!' He guided me to a seat in the parlour. 'I won't be a moment, now. I must attend to Mrs Jenkins here,' he said, pointing at the fallen woman. 'It's so wonderful to see you, Patrick. You must tell me all the news from Freetown!'

I was too stunned to talk, so I sat studying the collection of African masks on his walls until he returned.

'You really must forgive Mrs Jenkins, my housekeeper. She shouldn't be alarmed, but she always is. There are a few black faces in the parish nowadays. You'd think she'd grown accustomed to them. Only the other afternoon she was remarking on the arrival of another African on the green. A very strange fellow, she says, shabby and rough-looking. She says you reminded her of him, but then she thinks you all look alike, when, of course, as we both know, nothing could be further from the truth, could it?'

He guided me into the house by my shoulders, steering me around the housekeeper.

'Your father is a wonderful man, Patrick. Your dear departed mother was also a very special woman.'

'Sir, my name is not Patrick. It is Jupiter. Patrick was my older brother. He is dead. And my father is very well, thank you.'

'What is that you say? Patrick – dead? Oh how awful. And how terrible for your parents. He was such a special child. How did he die, may I ask?'

'He had an accident on the river. He drowned.'

'But he was a sturdy lad, he knew the rivers well. How strange.'

'He fell over a waterfall.'

'I see. Here, let me help you with your bag, Jupiter. Please do sit down. The hour is late, but Mrs Jenkins will prepare some tea and cakes, won't you, Mrs Jenkins?' he said to the keyhole.

Mrs Jenkins carried in a tray with tea, oatcakes and a copy of the *Public Advertiser*.

I will never understand the habit of drinking this hot, brown, bitter water. I sugared it, added milk, and allowed the monkey to sip away to his heart's content.

'And what brings you here, Jupiter?'

'My father gave us your name as a man we could depend on should trouble befall us.'

'I hope I merit his trust. What trouble is it that brings you unannounced to my door?'

'Trouble of the very worst kind, sir. I am a student at the African Academy in Clapham. I believe my younger brother, Robert, is missing. He had been invited to visit Sir Thomas Manton with a friend of his. They never arrived, and I believe they have been kidnapped by highwaymen very near here, on the Stratford road, a few days ago. I must find him.'

'I had heard rumours of such a thing. I had thought it idle gossip.'

'We must make our way to Sir Thomas's house without delay.'

'Why, of course we must, my boy! Is the school aware of your absence?'

My silence disturbed him.

'I will write to them this instant and send a rider across the river tonight to let them know where you are. This is most irresponsible behaviour. Patrick would never have done such a thing. You will excuse me while I pen a swift message.'

He stamped out of the room muttering words like 'disgraceful', 'absurd', and 'shocking behaviour' just loudly enough for me to hear.

The monkey, having finished the oatcake, was wiping his mouth with a napkin. I picked up the newspaper and fanned myself with it. I fanned the monkey, and when that got boring I rolled up the paper and tried to tap it softly on the head. The monkey was fast, of course, and flew to safety on top of a cupboard. I settled down and scanned the paper. It made very little sense to me, but Robert loved this sort of thing: reports from the Court of St James about Sir Somebody-or-other being appointed a sheriff or privy councillor, ambassadors from God-alone-knows-where having private audiences with His Majesty, and wars and more wars all over the world, apparently. I turned the sheet over, hoping for something more lively, but there were only advertisements for the cargoes of newly-arrived ships and rich men's bits and pieces.

The last entry in the paper brought me to my feet.

For Sale: A well-made black boy about twelve years of age, speaks good English, and is apt to make a useful houseboy under correct instruction. Answers to the name of Bobby. Enquiries to Mr Jacob Shelton at The Crown and Sceptre, Roman Road. To be sold the afternoon of twelfth January.

Bobby. It was Robert. I knew it was.

I rushed into Reverend Wilde's office.

'Have they not taught you how to knock at the academy?'

'It's Robert, Mr Wilde. This is Robert. This Bobby, here.' I flashed the paper in his face.

'Your behaviour is atrocious, Jupiter.' He snatched the *Public Advertiser* from me. 'I have a good mind to write to your father and tell him how our climate has led to a degradation of Sierra Leonean manners!' He sighed and read where I pointed. 'Oh, I see . . . Strange . . . I don't know.'

'It's him, sir. I'm sure of it. We have to go there now and rescue him!'

'First things first, young man. You'll need to sleep, and I will alert the constables tomorrow morning. Unfortunately this house has no room for another bed, but you may sleep here in this armchair, if it is agreeable to you.'

I had seen parish constables before. They were

usually old busybodies who had nothing better to do with their time than interfere in the affairs of their neighbours.

I knew in my bones that by tomorrow it would already be too late.

And as I pretended to sleep, I plotted my next move.

[17]

The fire was almost out in the grate. A handful of embers lit my way out of the room into the corridor. With great stealth, I took the heavy poker from the coal scuttle, wrapped it in rags and tied it on to my backpack. I padded into the corridor and tried the door knob to exit the house. It was locked. I stepped back into the front room and tried the window. Locked again. The old house creaked most loudly. I trod as carefully and quietly as I could to the kitchen at the rear of the house. I felt my way carefully in the darkness, shifting my weight judiciously as I went. I opened a drawer and felt about until I found what I was looking for: a small knife. I crept towards the door. A squeal loud enough to wake the entire parish rose from the floor. It was the monkey. I was standing on its tail. It continued to shriek and dash around, knocking breakable things in the darkness. I had to get out immediately before Reverend Wilde made it downstairs. I worked the knife in the lock. I did not know what I was doing, I'd only heard about this from one of the boys at the academy. Before long I heard a *hhcleheuengg!* and the door was open.

I remembered from the brown-paper map that Roman Road was very close. I kept to the shadows. This was a very empty district and I did not need to meet any more like Mrs Jenkins tonight.

I need not have worried about getting lost. I had only to follow my nose and ears. The eternal pub stink of spilt beer and gin, unwashed bodies and tobacco was unmisteakable. Screams, raucous laughter and a lone voice singing a sea shanty told me I was getting close. The Crown and Sceptre was a three-storey building set a small way off the road in its own courtyard. Its walls bulged outwards and were peeling. The thatched roof was covered with roughly-cut patches of incongruous woods.

I peeked through a window and saw drunkards were lying amidst the mayhem. Some were asleep in pools of their own urine and vomit.

I used the muffled poker to punch a hole in a basement window. I put my hand through the hole, turned the latch and slithered into the pub.

I heard a roar of agony from behind a door. It was Robert. I'd know that sound anywhere. It was the sound my little brother made when he was fighting against being beaten. It was the noise he made whenever I had occasion to beat him.

The door was ajar. Robert was pinned to a table by two bearded bullies.

'Don't burn his face, fool. Burn the feet. Underneath.'

Blood was on the floor and walls. In one corner, a body lay covered by a sack. From the shape of the head I knew it was William Tamba, and from its stillness I knew he was dead.

Before I could take the measure of anything, I found myself whacking the back of the first torturer with the poker. I struck him a very great many times very rapidly before turning on his terrified accomplice. The man sought to slip past me and escape. I cuffed him about the head, maybe twenty or so times, until he stopped moving and moaning.

Robert, brave boy, was already working himself off the bench. His wide-staring eyes were wet. He smiled with his mouth alone. I covered him with a shirt I found in the corner. It was too small for him and blood from cuts to his back and chest quickly soaked into it. Wordlessly, he squeezed himself into a pair of breeches. I struggled to help him fasten them but his waist was too large.

'Breathe in, Robert,' I commanded.

It was hard work for him. He was in some pain and was swallowing sobs to stop from crying aloud.

'Try again, you must, brother, breathe in, there we go, there we go, there—!'

Voices and footsteps were on the stairwell. Loud, drunken voices singing. Stumbling boots, hard and heavy. And another unmistakeable sound. The rattle of chains. And as they stumbled they sang:

> *''Tis to Amerikee we do be bound*
> *With darkies for to sell-o*
> *On Guinea's coast my fortune's found*
> *Farewell, my love, farewell-o.'*

When the door opened I was ready. There were two of them. I reached through the opening and pulled the first fellow towards me. He was tiny and I flung him against the wall. His head made the noise: *bhlookuk*. His mate was very much larger and jumped forward to circle me with a machete in one hand and a dagger in the other. Every time I moved, he would jab or swipe at me until I was backed into a corner. I could see no way past him. I started to kick wildly, hoping to unbalance him, but he was fast, very fast. It was only when I stood breathless and shaking, wedged into the corner, that I felt blood leaking warmly from where the machete had nicked both legs. As he drew back the larger blade to run me through, I repeated the name of Our Lord and Saviour and glanced around for my brother, that his face should be my last sight on Earth.

I had never heard a blunderbuss fire so close to me before. I had never seen a head explode before. It was whipped away from the shoulders in a dense spray of pellets that very nearly took my own head too. The man's body remained standing for a moment or two while blood spouted from its neck. Then it collapsed and fell into my arms. I shrieked but couldn't hear my own screams. The gun's discharge had deafened me. Throwing the corpse aside, I noticed Robert feverishly reloading the gun from a cabinet full of ammunition. He was saying something I couldn't hear. That strange smile was still on his face. He motioned towards the cabinet at some pistols. I could see they had already been loaded. I grabbed them and signalled for him to follow me out of the door.

The stairs were blocked by a crowd of crazed, bad-smelling men coming to seek the source of the gunfire. Robert showed it to them and fired another storm of pellets at their terrified faces. It was not a pretty sight, although some of them didn't look any worse for it, to be honest. More frightening still was the way Robert bashed through the fallen using the butt of the blunderbuss. He was like a madman, hitting out wildly at everything in his path. I had to pull him away with one hand while firing one pistol up the stairs to deter anyone from closing in on us. If we made it to the corridor we could be away before they gathered their forces. My legs started to hurt from the cuts inflicted by the machete. Running would be difficult. Robert was limping from his wounds as well, but I noticed that was wearing a pair of bright green gold-buckled shoes that he'd somehow taken from someone during the fight. Clever Robert! I hauled over a side-table to jam under the door to the drinking parlour.

The back door was open. It gave on to farmland and a few outhouses. The night air felt clear, frosty and welcoming. We ran for it. A stout-bodied, bearded man turned from just outside the garden door to block our escape. He was holding a huge woodman's axe. I levelled the remaining pistol at him and pulled the trigger. Nothing happened. I saw the axeman laughing as he stepped towards us. I would have to wrest the weapon from him. It wasn't going to be easy. He looked very adept and at ease with it. I would have to get inside the swing of the axehead and grasp the handle, then we could be on more equal terms and I would have a height advantage. But that was also a problem. I'd have to crouch to get level with his hands and that would make me a bigger, slower target.

I felt, more than heard, the roar of curses gathering from the pub's main room and the accompanying thud of some kind of battering ram. They'd be on us in an instant.

The axeman raised the axe above his head, snarled, then suddenly stopped as if under some spell. His eyes crossed and then, with the weapon still held high, he fell backwards like a fallen tree.

We wasted no time and hurried out into the night before our pursuers came through the door. We were in the middle of nowhere. There were no lights anywhere.

'This way, my brothers, this way!' The rasping voice cutting through our impaired hearing belonged to a black man. We could make him out now, behind one of the cowsheds. He was beckoning us to follow him. We moved as quickly and quietly as we could.

18

The man ran ahead of us, guiding us through the gardens and side-alleys skirting the fields, until we arrived, exhausted and half frozen, at a very crude little shelter, hardly more than a lean-to windbreak amongst folded-up market stalls. We crawled in and made ourselves at home.

It was somewhat disconcerting when the man reached out and slapped us on the shoulders and pinched our cheeks. Our hearing had improved and we heard the most atrocious laugh gurgling at the base of his throat. Being unable to see, it was impossible to tell if he was expressing joy or murderous intent. For some reason I thought of the ogres, trolls and goblin-folk that are rumoured to haunt this island, and I remembered hearing of how they could change appearance to lure their prey into their underworld lairs.

I banished these thoughts and watched the stranger set to work, sparking a tinderbox over a stub of candle. He was no shapeshifter. Our saviour was slightly stooped and grey-haired. He had a patch over his left eye and a squint in his right. He wore an old navy greatcoat a few sizes too big for him. It smelt mouldy. He sat on the damp earth rocking back and forth, smiling to himself and saying. 'Yes, yes, yes, yes, yes, yes, yes!'

I caught Robert's eye and saw the alarm in his face and the used pistol he was holding like a club under his shirt.

'Yes, yes, yes, together, together!' The man's voice was like pee on hot coals. He was clearly mad and we would need to dump him as soon as possible to make good our escape.

I put my hand to my pocket, feeling for a few coins.

'Thank you, my friend. You have risked your life for ours. Allow me to offer you some small token of our appreciation.'

The strength of his grip on my elbow was appalling. I could not move my arm. His other hand gripped Robert in a similar fashion.

'You don't see, do you? Money is good, very good. But you need your people more. You need your own people most of all. Do you understand? Your own people!'

I whipped my arm from his grasp and pulled Robert closer to me. An odd smile played across the stranger's face and he appeared to wipe tears from his eyes.

'You saw the man with the axe? You saw how he fell?' The lunatic fixed me with his one-eyed gaze. 'Have you ever seen someone fall like that before? Straight over and gone?'

'That was extraordinary,' I admitted. 'How did you accomplish it?'

He laughed his unbearable laugh once more. 'I did it the same way you did it. Don't you see, young one?'

I only saw a sad fool. But he had helped us and it was our duty to offer recompense to him in any way we could. I pushed the handful of coins at him again. Robert was uncharacteristically silent. He had let the pistol fall to the ground and was staring open-mouthed at our host.

'See what, sir? That we have just killed and wounded a handful of white rogues and will soon be hunted down and killed ourselves if you persist with this behaviour.'

'No. I thought you were sharper than this. Life in England has turned you soft. You just don't see at all. You can't. You have forgotten.' He turned aside and started weeping very softly.

'Who are you to speak to me in this manner! Forgotten what, fool?'

'Forgotten *me*, Jupiter!'

Beneath the grey skin and hair something surfaced. I felt suddenly giddy and almost lost my balance. The wretch seemed to grow in front of me. His shoulders swelled, his voice deepened. I feared I was losing my mind. I clutched Robert, and as I stood to leave the hovel I banged my head on its excuse for a roof. Only my faith in Christ saved me from seeing him as an evil spirit made flesh, or a duppy straight from the tales of terror with which the Jamaican boys used to keep us awake.

'You don't know me, do you, Jupiter?'

'How do you know my name?'

'This must be little Robby. Fine young man. Sharper than you. Maybe sharper than me, too. Tell him who I am, Robby, go on. I know you've guessed correctly.'

'Jupiter, this is Patrick. Our brother, Patrick. Back from the dead.'

I couldn't see it. Everything was wrong. I didn't want to see it. This shrivelled, hobbling, reeking madman could never be Patrick. And yet . . . and yet . . .

'Robert!' My voice sounded terrible. It was like a mouse squeaking. I was losing control of myself. 'Robert, what do you mean? What are you saying?'

'Show him,' Robert ordered the stranger. 'Show him how you felled the axeman.'

The rough-looking man extracted a slingshot from his greatcoat and laid it before me. The design, the materials, the marks betraying its style of use and evidence of its repair history and adaptation for various missiles showed that it was a weapon made by and for the person who taught me all I knew about slingshots. It was a Williams family weapon.

'Patrick, it can't be you! It can't be!' As I said the words, I realized I was wrong. It could be Patrick, or at least a withered, broken shadow of our older brother. He held out his arms to embrace me, and as he did so I was more confused, more scared and felt more alone than I have ever felt before or since.

'But you are dressed like a beggar, your hair is almost white.' I spoke to prevent him coming near me again. I spoke to stop myself understanding what was happening. 'I thought I . . . We all thought you were dead.'

'Patrick did die, Jupiter, many many times. You did not kill him, but others did. I am now a man, and I go by the name of Patch.' He glanced over his shoulder at the bubbling voices beyond the fence. 'We'd better go, Jupiter. We'll both carry Robert, one on each side.

When I say run, we run. When I say go, we go. When I say hide, we hide. Do you understand me?'

I did and I didn't.

I said, 'Yes, Patrick.'

We ran out into the cold and dark.

[19]

The door to the vicarage swung open at my touch. Furniture, books, papers, crockery and a dead monkey were scattered about the house. In the kitchen, the priest lay face down on the floor with his legs in the wrong positions. I've seen many dead people before, of course, but I've never seen an actual human brain. That is to say, parts of an actual human brain on the floor that have spilt from a crushed skull. Robert rushed away to vomit. I felt like joining him, but made the sign of the cross instead.

'What are you doing?' Patrick asked.

'I was commending his soul to God.'

'Oh, I see. How nice. Where does he hide his money?'

'I beg your pardon. His money?'

'Yes. You know?' He rubbed his forefingers together.

'How dare you? This was our father's friend.'

'I know. I remember him well. You do not. Now where did this nasty little man keep his treasure? It's still around somewhere, because whoever did this was not looking for money. They were looking for you!'

'This is beneath us. Let's away from here before the constables are summoned.'

'There'll be no beadles for a while yet. There's food here, and we can dress Robert's wounds. We'll eat, drink and be gone before he starts to stink.'

'My brother, we cannot prepare and eat food around the dead. There needs to be some decency.'

'Let the dead bury their own. Didn't your Jesus say that?'

Your Jesus? Being unable to comprehend what he meant by that outburst, I let him direct our gathering up of clothes, food and what loose change there was about the place.

Robert returned from his vomiting. 'Brother Patrick, I believe we should leave this house immediately.'

Patrick was stuffing his mouth with bread. 'Leave? Now? Why? It is warm here and you must wash the blood from your body and rest awhile before the next leg of our journey.'

'Next leg?' I asked. 'What next leg? We are going directly to the house of Sir Thomas Manton, where we shall give a full account of all that has occurred.'

Patrick had found a bottle of whisky and was swigging from it, drinking very long and very deep as if it was spring water. 'A full account.' He chuckled. 'A full account of your murders. A full account of your exploits away from the African Academy. Away from your lawful guardians . . . A full account of this?' He gestured about him. 'And which court of law in this country will believe you? You are murderers. We are murderers, all of us. Black murderers.'

'But Reverend Venn, Mr Stephen, Mr Macaulay, all of those gentlemen and many others can vouch for us against the word of these child-stealing reprobates from whom we've just escaped. And there is still our family name, the good standing of our father. How can you forget that? Surely the name of Williams still counts for something?'

'It counts for nothing, my dear brothers. Nothing at all.'

'What can you mean by this?' I shouted into his face. I had one hand ready to grab him by the neck and the other bunched to strike his face.

'Father is dead.' Patrick wiped a used plate with a piece of crust and sucked at it. 'Yes. Dead.'

'Daddy can't be dead.' I hadn't spoken of him as 'Daddy' since I was nine.

Robert came and stood beside me as if to face down Patrick.

'Daddy is waiting for us back in Freetown,' said

Robert. 'There's still our house, our houses, the family business, the ministry. All of that's still there, surely? Who can look after it, if not us?'

'Jupiter, you must attend more keenly to Robert's cultural education. He speaks like an English boy. So do you, now I think of it. My brothers, the family business went with Father. He died owing a great many people a great deal of money. Daddies die too, you know. Just like everyone else.'

'But my letters,' I insisted. 'I've been writing to him every week for almost a year. All the time we've been here.'

'And you've received how many replies, exactly, Jupiter?'

'One.'

'Hmm, yes, that would be about right.'

'But the post. It's dreadful between London and Freetown, isn't it?'

'Is it, really? How many letters do those Caulker boys get? One a month each, I'll bet. And their parents can only just read and write. Amazing that, isn't it? Jupiter – come back!'

But I was already out of the kitchen door and standing in the night. I couldn't let that monster who called himself my brother see my tears. I couldn't let Robert see them either.

* * *

Once upon a time in Africa, we buried Mommy. Daddy, Patrick, baby Robert and I buried her. We stood around the graveyard by the old Cotton Tree, dressed in the latest London fashion, looking like we were off to the opera. All Freetown turned out; natives, Maroons, and all of us from Nova Scotia. Everyone knew and loved Mommy. And as her casket was lowered into the earth I looked up and saw that Daddy was gazing at me, and the expression on his face was one that Mommy used to have. It was as if he had been waiting for me to look up and catch his eye. And he was smiling as if to let me know that everything was all right. That Mommy was talking through him from another place to let us know that everything was all right, and she'd still be there as long as Daddy, Patrick, Robert and I were there. And because Daddy wasn't sad, I wasn't sad. As long as Daddy and I were together, Mommy would be with us. All the stories of their meeting by chance as very young people, and their escape from slavery, of how they had to run away because they were slaves in love – because slaves were not supposed to love – and how Daddy became a soldier for Great Britain, so he could get the freedom for me to be born on the floor of a church in Canada rather than a slave cabin in Georgia. And how all four of us, Patrick, Daddy, Mommy and me made that long, cold, crazy, cramped trip from Canada to Sierra Leone. That promised land where nothing and nobody now waited for me.

Have you ever felt time stop? When I say 'to feel time stop' I don't mean those bored or anxious moments when seconds hang and drip like icicles. I'm not talking about those times when you explode with anger and jump into violence.

If you've really felt time stop, you'll know that there are no floods of tears and no screams or even confusion. Because time has stopped . . . like *this*.

And nothing happens!

A short, very high-pitched scream pulled me from my reflections and I rushed back inside. Robert and Patrick were packing up in a great hurry. 'It was some old woman,' Patrick said.

'What woman? Where?'

They pointed to the floor where a third body now lay. It was Mrs Jenkins, the housekeeper.

'Walked in the front door, took one look at me and just collapsed,' said Robert. 'You'd think she'd never seen a black face before.'

'Run,' Patrick commanded. 'Others will have heard

her noise. They'll be here soon.'

'We'll find shelter. I know a place in East Smithfield. We'll be safe there and we can look for a ship needing hands.'

'A ship needing hands? We are not sailors, Patrick!' said Robert.

'Every man is a seaman, as you will soon discover.'

'I was as sick as a crow on the journey here from Freetown.'

'Are you suggesting then that we travel back home overland?'

Robert and I looked at one another in silence.

'Then follow me. We will stay amongst friends tonight.'

'You have friends here?' I asked.

'What did I just say, Jupey-boy?'

'You said run,' I growled.

'So run, boy, run! And for your information, we are off to The Shovel.'

'The *what*?'

'The Shovel. Our people are there.'

[20]

We got lost a few times on the way to The Shovel, but it was Robert who eventually navigated our way from Bethnal Green to East Smithfield, just as the sun was rising. All the hours he had spent poring over maps finally served a purpose.

When we came in sight of the Tower of London, I knew we were in the same derelict parish from the night before. After a few turns, Patrick brought us to the door of The Shovel. It was, needless to say, yet another alehouse.

I had never met people like these before. In our travels we have met rough men, we have met poor men, low, mean and frankly stupid men, but never had I seen such a concentration of these qualities, not just in one place, but in each face that was presented to me.

They were men of all nations, some Mohammedans and Hindus, a Chinaman or two, the odd Dane or Irisher, but mostly sons of Africa. They had names like Beefy, Caractacus, Clebs and Dog-Rice. Many appeared to bear injuries of some description. One had no arms, legs, ears; another was legless. Some had splits cut in their noses, marking them as thieves. And Patrick was not the only one sporting an eyepatch.

The Shovel was incredibly busy. Sailors and dock workers of all kinds, as well as ne'er-do-wells, seemed to hover about the place. There was a storage area to the rear of the building where barrels, bales and bundles of goods rolled in and out at all hours. It smelt of tobacco, nutmeg and rum. Tears in the packaging revealed flashes of silk or starched cotton. The place was obviously well organised, but how and by whom was a complete mystery to me.

'You can't walk around here looking like that!' snapped Patrick.

Apart from some smudges and very slight tears, my clothes were in quite good condition. 'What's wrong with these clothes? Father paid a very great deal of money for them.'

'Those aren't the sort of clothes you wear around these parts. You'll stick out a mile. And besides, you will no doubt be surprised to learn that a fair few people can read in East Smithfield. They might not be so brotherly towards you when they see you fit the description of a murderer. Or a runaway. There's probably a reward bring printed up as we speak.'

'Then we must go to Sir Thomas Manton and explain everything to him without delay!'

'No, Jupiter. You're going to the barber immediately. You need a haircut and a change of clothes. Come!'

'Erm, Patrick?' Robert began. 'Jupiter does have a point. If we continue running now . . . if we don't contact some men of good standing who'll believe us, then we are doomed to run from the law for the rest of our lives.'

'That is correct.'

'What about my studies . . . our studies?'

Patrick looked at him the way you'd look at a baby playing with a razor.

'We run, brothers. Do you still think we're in Sierra Leone? Our name means nothing here, while this,' he stroked the skin of his cheek, 'means everything. To the barber. Now!'

'This is my friend, Society.' Patrick pulled a short, miserable-looking fellow towards us. 'Society, here, will look after you. Anything you want or need – he'll arrange it for you. You can trust him absolutely.'

Society looked wrong. It wasn't that he looked miserable (which he did), or that he had tiny clouds of flies around him even though it was deepest winter, or that instead of rising to shake our hands he grunted at us questioningly and continued to rock back and forth on the balls of his feet. No, lots of people have strange ways. Society was wrong in a way I couldn't put my finger on. A bad way. It started to make sense when he moved off to order drinks. Even uncoordinated people have some pattern to their movements. Society had none whatsoever.

'He's also the house barber,' Patrick informed us. 'One of many skills you possess, eh, Society?'

'Yes, Patch. I have many skills. Many skills, as you know! I am pleased to meet these members of your family. Your brothers, eh?' He stroked his chin, said 'Fresh blood!' very loudly and laughed.

I found him difficult to like.

'And one more thing, Jupiter,' said Patrick. 'The money!'

'What money?'

'The money that Father would have given you to hide away as a reserve in case of emergencies – such as this. The money that you would not have left the academy without. Where is it?'

'I have it here. It is quite safe.'

'How much?'

'Some ten pounds, give or take a few shillings.'

'Give it to me.'

'It is my money, Patrick, and I shall decide how it shall be spent.'

'Wrong, brother. The money belongs to all of us, and I am best placed to look after it. You may not have noticed, but not everyone here is as trustworthy as Society. There are those here who make a living from nurturing confidence and turning untruths. Beware!' He held out his hand and I gave over almost all the money we had in the world to him.

Our heads were shaved to the scalp. We were given bandanas to wear. Our good clothes were exchanged for rags. Oily rags, which still had the smell of other people on them. When they came for my shoes I was obliged to throw a punch or two. I refused to surrender them. When two thin wooden blocks with leather straps were presented to me, I knocked them away. There was no way I'd surrender my good shoes for those half-clogs. I would never be shoeless in this world. My shoes were handmade, and I was all too aware of the money Father had spent on them.

After a short, nasty struggle with Society, he relented and let me keep my footwear. The tone of his voice left me in no doubt that he thought I was an idiot and that I would find myself dead or in captivity before too long if I continued to wear those shoes in East Smithfield. I did not care. They could take my coat, my neckerchief, my hair, and even my pride, but not my shoes. Never. They were, quite literally, what I was worth.

I can say without fear of contradiction that that house was the most filthy abode I have ever slept in. Vermin abounded. As we fell to our beds of sacking, so did the fleas and mites fall to drink our blood and eat our skin. Comfort was impossssible. Rats vied with us for living space in the attic. They scrambled along the roof beams, showering us with droppings, and sometimes fat, quarrelling knots of them tumbled down to challenge us directly. I slept with a covering over my head. I felt them rumbling beneath the thin floorboards. All I will say of the privy is that it was frothing with poo-covered rodents and I contained myself for the duration of my stay there.

A stable would have been preferable, at least then I would have been spared the inane and constant chatter of our roommates. For over three hours of that dreadful night an argument prevailed over whether Jesus was the true god of kings or the true king of gods. I believe one of the debaters was a scholar, for he used the words 'epistemology' and 'reductionist' correctly.

He was ultimately defeated by the following tirade of patois from one of the company: 'Well, if 'im nah know dat 'im nah know, den 'im nah know 'im nah know, right? So 'ow 'im know dat 'im nah know dat 'im nah know, if 'im nah know dat 'im nah know 'im nah know, eh? Dyamn fool!' On which point of impeccable logic we, rats and all, fell to exhausted, blessed sleep through the remaining two hours before daybreak.

One thing that could be said in favour of our new home was that the food was absolutely delicious. Patrick said we could eat as much as we wanted. His 'bucko mates' would carry the cost, he assured us.

So we ate.

I had never tasted such wonderful food, or even imagined that it would be available, in this country. We had an old Royal Navy cook from Mauritius living with us and because we were right by the docks we had fish and meat of all kinds in great abundance. In the first three days we ate roast cod with green banana mash and gravy, peppered crab soup with greens and dumplings, and a beef curry with English winter vegetables and rice. At all times of the day or night two or three spits loaded with seasoned ducklings, chickens and quail, would be turning. We helped ourselves to the smaller game birds at our leisure as we walked about the building. There was pepper sauce from Scotch Bonnet peppers at The Shovel as well! Good-quality sugar cane and pineapples stood in for the stodgy steamed puddings we had endured at the African Academy.

We didn't see very much of Patrick for the first night. I knew already not to ask him about his business. I passed the time in treating and bandaging the wounds on Robert's back. He absolutely refused to talk about what happened to him in the cellar of The Crown and Sceptre. I would not press him on the matter.

He would speak when he was ready.

The next morning, Patrick shook us awake and whispered that we should follow him to the storeroom. 'My brothers, you must not leave this house for any reason – *any* reason – unless I command you to do so!' he instructed. 'There is talk in the taverns hereabouts of a tall, silent stranger travelling around handing out notices of a handsome reward for two boys such as yourselves.'

Robert and I exchanged an anxious glance.

'They say he is a very dangerous man. A terribly violent man. He has been fighting his way through the docks like a man possessed.'

'We know this person, Patrick. His name is Bavya and what they say about him is true. He is to be feared,' said Robert.

'You are in very great danger then, even here! There are some under this roof who would sell their fellow Africans for a small price. You must swear to me that you will remain in The Shovel until it is time to depart. Swear it!'

We swore.

And so I devoted my energies towards trying to be a dutiful younger brother. I wanted to trust Patrick absolutely, the way I used to. But it was impossible. I didn't recognize this grey-haired bully, and he didn't recognize me.

21

Being cooped up in The Shovel was driving me insane. There was nothing to read in that building. There was no music save the mobbish *bangcarang* which shook the walls nightly. I had no wish to join the coarse assemblies of these people. They were a disgrace to our race. There were one or two fellows of good character who had fallen upon hard times, but the rest were layabouts and good-for-nothings. They did not seek to advance themselves or improve their station in any way. They were content to loaf around the quayside until they had drunk away or gambled their last coin. Beyond the colour of our skins we had nothing in common.

Of course, we did not stay inside that smelly pub. There was a world beyond its grubby windows and I was determined to explore it. Even though Bavya, or someone very much like him, had been sighted nearby, I had no doubt that Robert and I could outsmart the brute.

'Would you like to see the Tower of London, Robert?'

'I would like that very much, but we have been ordered not to leave this place. We have given our word.'

'True, we have. But in a sense, we are not really leaving this place. We can get a good look at the Tower from the end of the street. The Shovel will still be in view. We'll have gone no distance at all. It really is very close.'

'Very well, Jupiter. I'll just let Society know where we'll—'

'Er, no. I don't think he'll want to be disturbed by our comings and goings. He's a busy man with troubles enough. Come on, let's go. We'll only be five minutes.'

We strolled to the top of East Smithfield and looked across a stretch of bustling streets. There it was, in all its glory – the Tower of London!

Robert was clearly in awe. He couldn't stop talking. He started to lecture me on how the Tower was built by William the Conqueror, all about Anne Boleyn's execution, Guy Fawkes' interrogation, the Royal Armoury and all sorts of things. I let him talk and listened respectfully. I had forgotten what good company he could be for one of his years.

'Would you like a closer look, brother?'

'No, we should stay close to The Shovel, really.' He

looked about him and noticed the masts and sails of ships bobbing in the docks nearby. 'Although I would truly like to have a look at some of those. They're practically on our doorstep, aren't they?'

We scooted off down an alley, stepped across a muddy courtyard, pushed our way through a very crowded side-street where entire families seemed to be at work and play, before crossing a major road and down another alley, only to realize that we were lost.

There was no sign of any mast or sail, no sign of anything I could recall. The whole feel of this parish was different. It was still a very poor place, but it was drab. There was not the same feeling of chaos that was present around the docks. The people here dressed more soberly. There were no outlandish fashions. In fact, as we soon noticed, there were no outlanders. Everyone here was not just white and English, they also looked as if they were very closely related to each other. And it was very quiet.

'I think we should go back the way we came,' Robert suggested.

I looked over my shoulder and saw a whole series of alley-mouths leading off in different directions. 'Let's take this one,' I said, leading the way towards the nearest alley.

'Jupiter, that's the wrong one. Stop, you're going the wrong way!'

I was definitely going the *right* way, but as I took a number of turns the neighbourhood became even more strangely poor and plain.

'Where now?' Robert folded his arms and I waited for him to say *Jupiter, stupider*.

'I think we should assess our position on a full stomach. I'm hungry,' I said.

We followed the smell of cooked food to a bakery and looked through the window. We saw breads, cakes, puddings and all kinds of English stodge in the window. We also saw our reflections. We looked like common criminals – pirates to be precise.

'I think one of those pork pies will do nicely, don't you?' I asked.

Robert turned to me slowly. 'Jupiter, you lied to Patrick. You didn't give him all the money.'

'That anchovy sauce will go well with it, wouldn't you say?'

'Jupiter, Patrick needs the money to look after us. What are you up to?'

'I held back a few pounds, Robert. You see, until I know what Patrick's real intentions are, I'm looking after myself. That makes sense, doesn't it?'

Robert said nothing.

'Now how about that pie, eh?'

By way of a greeting the shopkeeper said 'Oh yeah?' when we entered his premises. He said it again, followed by 'Wodjewonteh?'

'That rather tasty-looking pie in your window, if you don't mind, sir!' I pointed at it and saw that a crowd of very young boys had gathered to stare at us. There were many of them and they must have been following us silently.

'A pie?'

'Yes, please.'

'A pork pie?'

We nodded.

He placed the food on the counter and named a price.

'Would you wrap it for us, please?'

He wrapped it roughly.

I handed over a pound note.

'You must be jokin'! You're 'avin me on, ain't ya? Comin' in 'ere, cleanin' me out of change this time of the day. Wodjewplainateh?'

I collected the change (which was a huge pile of small coins), and left the shop. The crowd of boys had vanished. We ate as we walked.

'This way,' said Robert. I followed him.

He stopped suddenly and faced me.

'Do you want to know what happened to me and William Tamba at that pub, in that cellar? What they were doing to me?' His voice was suddenly thick and heavy.

'You can tell me. I'm your brother. You should tell someone, at least.'

'They mark you, Jupiter. They mark you. Sometimes with a knife, sometimes with a hot iron. They mark you to show that you belong to them. If you are sold on to someone else, I hear you are given a collar to wear. Sometimes it's silver, sometimes it's brass. But you are always marked. William was brave. He fought them. When they tried to cut him, the knife must have gone into his throat. He bled to death. That made them very angry. They had lost money. A dead black boy fetches no price. Out of spite and rage, they burnt me. And they cut me too.'

'Oh my God! My dear God. Robert!'

'It sounds worse than it was. I'm all right really. They didn't hurt me that much. Not in my body anyway . . .'

I put my hand about his shoulder, and had it not been for the embarrassment it would have caused him,

I would have carried him back to The Shovel in my arms like a baby.

As we turned, a pair of voices shouted, 'Boo! Yes you, boo, boo, boo, you, booboo!'

It was the layabouts from the river stairs who had laughed at me as I hopped to keep warm. They were still wearing their red scarves, but they were accompanied by three others, similarly dressed.

Robert was trembling. 'Who are they, Jupiter?'

'Riverbank ruffians. I'm amazed they recognized me. Apparently we all look the same to those that don't know us.'

'It's the shoes, Jupiter. The shoes. You should have changed them.'

This was no time to debate the issue. 'Robert. You are to stay behind me at all times. And say nothing.' I put my hands behind my back and addressed the young men.

'Sirs, I take it you are local to these parts?'

'What are you doin' 'ere?' said the most vocal rogue.

'We are enjoying a very good pork pie with anchovy sauce, and a stroll.'

'You shouldn't come round 'ere. You're not Blackgang boys, are you?'

I told him we were not.

'Well you're dead then.' He tugged a sharpened hammer from his waistcoat. 'C'mon lads!'

They all had sharpened hammers.

'Jupiter! What are we going to do?'

Behind my back, I had discreetly wriggled a hand into my backpack, loosened my slingshot, and was feeling for the familiar holes of a whistle lob when the charge came. I quickly took position and let the whistle lob fly high. Its terrible shriek brought them to a standstill as they tried to locate the source of the sound. It soared like an angel of destruction over their heads and smashed into the window of the bakery, shattering its glass with an equally splendid sound.

If we hadn't had to run for our lives at that point I would have jumped for joy. It was almost a shame to lose such a beautiful missile on scoundrels like these. I pushed Robert ahead of me as I ran. When I wasn't pushing him I was reloading the slingshot with a simple, heavy stone. I kept a second in reserve.

We left the maze of backstreets and came on to a green.

'We'll take them on here, Robert. Stay behind me!'

The first of the gang to boil out on to the green took a stone directly to his face. The impact seemed to lift him off his feet. The second to exit suffered a similar fate. I had a third stone ready and was peering along the street looking for more attackers. None came.

'Let's go!' I guided Robert in what I hoped was the right direction and walked backwards, making sure we weren't being followed.

'I know where we are!' Robert declared. 'This is Ratcliffe Highway! If we carry straight on down there, we'll be back at The Shovel in no time at all!'

'Are you quite sure now?'

'Very sure. Look, that is the church of St George-in-the-East. And down there, see them, see the masts? That's back to the docks we were looking at before.'

He was right and we set off down the road at great speed. We did not get very far before I felt a sudden sharp pain in my back and a metallic clank on the cobbles behind me.

The red-scarf rogues were back, and they had brought several more of their colleagues with them. I stopped counting after nine. Most of them were fully-grown men. I looked on the ground and saw a hammer. They had *throwing hammers*. They flourished and juggled them with casual expertise.

'You!' A very adult person stepped forward, pointing at me. 'You put my boy, Jack, on the floor, you black swine. You hurt my son, now I'm gonna hurt you.'

The pain in my back almost stopped me from moving. The sound of footsteps told me that yet more people, onlookers or otherwise, had encircled us. We were grabbed from all sides and pressed to the ground.

'You see this?' The man struck the earth twice with his hammer. 'See this? I'm gonna break every bone in your body with this. It's sharp, you see. *Sharp!* Hold 'em down. I'll start on the littl' un first.'

Two shots rang out. They sounded like pistols, very close. Our enemies were muttering, 'Blackgang, Blackgang, it's the Blackgang boys.'

'Release those boys, Freddie Franklin!' The voice was Patrick's. 'Release those boys *now*!'

'Can't do that, Patch! It's my son, they've hurt 'im bad. He's in a dreadful way. Can't move, nuffink. I'll take my revenge right here.'

'If your honour has been offended then we shall repay you in full, but you cannot harm these boys.'

'But they're not Blackgang, look at 'em.'

'No, they are not Blackgang. They are my brothers.'

'Your brothers?' The grip on my arm loosened and a knee in my back was lifted. 'I don't know about this, Patch. What are we gonna do? I can't walk away from this with nothing.'

'You won't, Freddie. On my honour. On my word.

I will sort something out.'

'You'd better sort it out, Patch. Cos, if you don't, I'll have that boy, I swear. Don't care if he's your brother or not. I'll take 'im and I'll make 'im pay in blood. You know I will. So sort it out soon!'

The crowd parted and our brother stepped through to help us to our feet. Beyond the crowd were four familiar faces from The Shovel. One of them was Society's. They all carried firearms.

'Patrick, thank you,' I whispered as we departed.

'Don't say a word.' He spoke through clenched teeth. 'Don't talk to me, Jupiter. You have no idea what trouble you have caused this day. If we were not related I would have left you to face the hammers of those rascals. Do not dare speak to me again this day!'

We followed his hunched shoulders all the way back to East Smithfield.

[22]

'All I asked was that you obey a simple command: do not leave The Shovel!'

Patrick had been pacing up and down the attic room for what seemed like hours. His rage was limitless. 'This is the real London! This is not your fancy African Academy. This is how people, real people, live in this city.'

I rose instantly. 'Patrick, I apologize most deeply for the distress I have brought you today!'

'Jupiter, will you please be quiet!' I sat. 'You don't know what you are talking about. Distress? Distress? Boy, you have nearly ruined my reputation and the name of this house and all who live here, and by extension, every other free dark-skinned person who lives east of the Tower. You don't understand anything, do you? We all rise and fall as one. We may not all be friends in this house, but we will always behave like family. Here we live by the speed of our wits and the strength in our arms. Badges of rank and friends in high places mean nothing. Nobody here knows or cares for your Mr

William Wilberforce or your Mr Granville Sharp. Many don't even know where Clapham is, let alone Sierra Leone. You are no longer Jupiter Williams – forget him, forget all that. You are a black now, a negro, a nigger, a blackamoor. That is who you are here.'

I rose again. 'Patrick, I respect you as my older brother and I confess I have no idea what happened to you after the incident at the waterfall, but I will never, *never* disgrace the name of Williams. I will never forget who I am or where I came from.'

'The name of Williams, eh? Do they teach history at that fool-school you went to? The name of Williams, *pah*! How do you think we got the "name of Williams"? All that means is that some white man who once owned our grandparents put his name on us. Like dogs. And now we are free, we still wear the name with pride.'

'I am not ashamed of our name. If you are no longer a Williams, how do you call yourself?'

'I told you before. I'm Patch. And yes, I know, I know, Patch is also a dog's name, but it is one of my own choosing.'

'What happened to you, Patrick?'

'I will tell you some day, but not now. I'm not sure you're ready to hear it.'

I felt he was waiting for me to beg him to tell his tale, but I would not give him the satisfaction.

'Jupiter, I am taking Robert to help me with a piece of work that needs doing in Shadwell this evening. You will remain here and you will not leave this house for any reason whatsoever.'

'Robert? Why are you taking him?'

'He's a useful young man. Knows more than most twice his age. True, he's not a natural fighter, but he's versatile, and a fast learner. And small!'

He slammed the door as he left.

23

The next five days were the longest of my life. When I wasn't helping the cook or the cellarman, I tried to be sociable. I tried to make friends, but most people in the house shunned me. As a result of my escapades on the Ratcliffe Highway, a lot of money left the house in an effort to restore goodwill with the offended gang. The only people who had time for me were Society, who watched me like a hawk, and the mad philosophy crew who were only too pleased to welcome new blood into their holy wars. There was a handful of unbelievers in the group and they started on me during an argument about Noah and the ark. Their irreverence was extraordinary. They wanted to know if woodpeckers were on the ark, and if so, what were the conditions of their storage. How did polar bears get on the ark? What animals did the lions eat? Who cleaned up after all those animals in a boat that must have been the size of Clapham Common. I know how big it was because I calculated it in the heat of a debate (which I lost) about the fact that if the ark took one hundred and twenty years to build, most of the wood would have rotted away by the time it took to the waters. I lost all my arguments, but I kept going back to them. I was bored beyond all imagination.

I hardly saw Robert, and when I did, I did not like what I saw. He would appear in the early hours of the morning and collapse on his sacking beside mine. He stank of strong drink. The short time he did spend in the house was in the company of Patrick and The Shovel's inner circle, where I was definitely not welcome. They were a bad lot, I could see that now. They gambled incessantly, and once when I went down to use the water pump, I saw him shaking and casting a cup of dice. He looked at me boldly, as if to say 'and what of it?' He was learning songs of the coarsest kind and on the second night he crashed to his pallet reeking not only of drink, but also of perfume. He slept with a smile on his face that night. In fact a smile was on his face throughout our stay at The Shovel. I strongly suspected that Patrick had introduced our little brother to a world of the most impure connections. I had to speak to Robert immediately, and correct his behaviour if it was within my power to do so.

On the third night, (or perhaps it was the fourth morning, as the whole house seemed to be sleeping), I heard the inner circle return to the pub. They were laughing and hooting loudly enough to wake the whole street. I listened to them in the main room downstairs. They were opening bottles of something or other and a dice cup was being shaken. I knew when it was Robert's turn on the dice because he had developed a high-pitched comic cackle which entertained his new friends as much as it disturbed me. The game must have been very brief because soon I heard two pairs of footsteps walk into the laundry room. Water was drawn and the sound of a washboard in use carried upstairs. Patrick and Robert broke into a tuneless chant of truly vile references to a maiden's honour.

I went down to see what was going on.

They were both bare-chested and kneeling before a fire, washing their shirts in a basin. The flames lit up a pattern of scars on Patrick's back. It looked like burnt rubber. When he saw me looking at it, he turned away.

'Where have you two been? What have you been doing all this time?'

'A deed without a name!' chirped Robert.

I didn't know what he was talking about, but it made Patrick howl with laughter.

'Jupiter, go back to sleep!'

I glared at them and, at a loss for anything to say, I

went, with immense sadness, back to my horrid little pallet and sacking bed, where I sat on my own and listened to their splashing and shouting.

When the noise stopped, I tiptoed back to the washroom. Their shirts had been hung out to dry on a rack before the fire. I looked into the basin. It may well have been a trick of the firelight, but the water looked red to me.

I cornered Robert the following afternoon. He looked like he hadn't slept. He was rocking very slowly from side to side. His mixture of smiles and smells was worrying. He was wearing a shirt so white it wasn't just clean, but brand new. All his clothes were new.

'Why have you forsaken me, my brother?' I asked.

'I haven't forsaken you, Jupiter. I am still here. We are still a family,' he slurred.

'Why do you do this?' I waved a hand around him. 'I did not risk my life to save you simply to see you fall prey to these spirit-eating wretches.' I lowered my face to his ear. 'We will leave this place as soon as we possibly can. If we make it to Sir Thomas Manton's house I am still sure—'

'What about Patrick?'

'Patrick! He has brought nothing but disaster upon

us since he appeared. Look at us now, near-vagabonds living amongst the lowest of the low.'

'We are so very far from being the lowest of the low in this house, Jupiter. Don't you understand that? Don't you understand anything?'

'How dare you speak to me like that! Apologize at once!'

'I am sorry, Jupiter. But I am not wrong. You need to see more of this city to see just how far down you can go.'

'You are a thief now, is that right? Patrick and his crew, they steal, don't they?'

'We take only what belongs to us.'

'What do you mean by that?'

'Ask him when you see him. He'll be here soon.'

'And you are enjoying all of this?'

'Very, very much so.' He hugged himself.

'How do you think Father would feel if he was alive to see you like this?'

'I believe he would have been proud and he would have understood perfectly what we are doing here.'

I grabbed him by the collar and flung him against the wall. 'You will never speak of our father in such a way again.'

He started to cry and I was immediately sorry for what I had done.

‘Father was right about you, you know.’

‘What are you saying now? Talk sense, boy!’

‘He was right about you. He said you changed. When you came back that time without Patrick. You were never the same person afterwards. That you became hard. That you stopped laughing. He said he could never talk to you after that. That you never listened to anyone.’

‘He said that? To *you*?’

Robert nodded and wiped a sleeve under his nose. ‘It was like he had lost two sons, he said. And it’s true. You don’t listen to anyone else and you think you know everything. The only time you laughed in years was that time when you hit Mr Unwin.’

‘He spoke about me to you?’

‘Who else could he speak to, Jupiter? Who else was there?’

[24]

Days and nights drifted into each other at The Shovel and only the tolling of bells on all sides told me that it was the Lord's day. After a light breakfast I returned to the attic to find it empty. I took the opportunity to enjoy some quiet moments with the Almighty. I took the pocket Bible I'd been given when leaving the school and flicked through to my favourite psalms. Then I knelt, facing the direction of St Katharine's church, where the bells tolled the loudest, and, with hands clasped lightly around the Bible, began to pray as I had been taught: 'Our father, who art in heaven, hallowed be thy name . . . forgive us this day our trespasses as we forgive those that trespass against us—'

'And lead us not into temptation. But deliver us from evil. A-men to that, Jupiter! A-men to that.' It was Society.

'What is the meaning of this? How dare you interrupt a man at prayer!'

'Are you a man? Was that a prayer?' He snatched the Bible from me and threw it across the room. I had never seen such extreme blasphemy before. I was too stunned to move.

'Forget that nonsense. You're coming with me. Your brother wants to show you something.'

'I will finish my prayers first.'

'You can pray where we're going.'

'What do you mean?'

'We are going to church. To a real church. Patch is already there waiting for us. In the congregation. He thinks you might be ready for a real church.'

The building Society ushered me into looked like no church I had ever seen before. It was off a courtyard in Whitechapel, and up some stairs above what seemed to be the premises of a builder's merchant.

There was a single, large, high-ceilinged room. It was full of people, some sitting, some standing. Most of them were very poor-looking and English. I spotted my brothers sitting close to the small platform from which the preacher spoke. The sermon had already started. Nonetheless, small crowds still chattered amongst themselves. The preacher was a short man of mixed race who spoke with a strong Jamaican accent. The subject was clearly freedom. As he spoke, the congregation passed a large basket amongst themselves. It was full of small loaves, and all present partook and passed it on, saying the words 'Bread of Freedom' as they did so.

'What place is this, Society? There seems to be no order of service. Are there to be no hymns? None here are dressed for worship. Is this some congregation of thieves? What god is worshipped here?' I asked, allowing my voice to rise on the last question.

Patrick hushed me and told me to settle and wait. He passed me the basket. 'Bread of Freedom, Jupiter.'

I declined.

'You must take the Bread of Freedom, and pass it along. Bread of Freedom, my brother.'

I took a loaf and passed the basket on as ordered. The bread tasted as gritty and half baked as I imagined it would.

'If liberty is not for all, then it is for none, is that not so?' declared the preacher.

The crowd assented.

'How free is the banker with beggars at his gate? Is that freedom?'

'Nooo!'

'Freedom is the natural state of man. But there is no knowing how sweet and right it is until it is taken away from you by force; until you have chafed under the yoke of slavery, 'til you have felt the slavemaster's whip sear your skin. Then, and only then can the divine nature of freedom be known. For Christ desires us to be free; and those who at this moment are subjected to the most villainous inhumanity on the plantations across the sea, in the Caribbean and in North America – they are as much your brothers and sisters in Christ as any of your neighbours who want for bread. Some of them, some who have known human bondage, are here amongst us today.'

All eyes turned to look at the handful of black people dotted about the room. I glared back at them: who were they to presume my status?

'Let us hear from them,' the preacher continued. 'Come forward, my brothers. Step forward and share the stories of your journeys to freedom!'

I thought for one terrible moment that he was pointing at me when he raised his forefinger, but he was summoning Society.

'My brother, Society, tell us your tale.'

Society stepped up to the stage. 'Brothers and sisters, I was once a slave on the island of Barbados. There I worked like an animal, worse than an animal, for a master as cruel as Satan himself.'

'And where did you labour, brother Society?'

'On the Codrington plantation, good reverend.'

'And who were your masters?'

'They are well known to all here. They were the Church of England.'

Gasps and a small cry swept the room.

'The Church, you say?' prompted the preacher.

'Yes, the Church of England. We were bought and sold by the Society for the Propagation of the Gospels in Foreign Lands. They own my people still in Barbados.'

'And how did you come by your name, sir?'

Society removed his overcoat, waistcoat and shirt. His back was covered with the same crosshatching of raised welts I glimpsed on my brother's back that night they laundered by firelight. On his chest, clearly visible, was the branded word: SOCIETY.

'That's how they treat us. They brand us like cattle, and beat us much worse.'

'And how did you escape these torments?'

'My work was as a cooper. I made barrels for the keeping of molasses. I built a barrel with a hiding space large enough for me to curl into. With help I was rolled on to a London-bound merchant ship and remained hidden, feeding off molasses, for two days, until I reckoned we were far enough away from Barbados for me to reveal myself. I was lucky, although the ship's captain wanted to sell me on for his own profit, his officers, seeing I knew some carpentry and was willing to learn, allowed me to work my passage here and turned a blind eye when I jumped ship.'

'Thank you, brother Society. Your tale will live in the hearts of us all, I am sure. There are other stories here, I know. Come, brother Patch, speak. Tell us of your journey to freedom. Tell us what freedom really means.'

I was transfixed and my head began to swim as my elder brother took to the platform beside the Jamaican.

'My story is different. I was a free man in Africa. I came from a family of traders. Good people. Christian people. I came into slavery through a terrible accident.'

At that moment, I inhaled for the first time since he mounted the platform.

'I fell into fast-flowing water during a journey far inland. I was swept over a waterfall. My life began again from the moment I hit that chute of water.'

He stared unblinkingly at me while he spoke.

'I must have been unconscious for hours, for when I came to I found myself clinging to a tree trunk floating down the river towards a place called Shenge. I ended up – I don't know how long later – on an island at the mouth of the river by the beach. I must have been close to death. The place was deserted. I ate raw crab meat for what seemed like seven days and nights. At last I saw a small lighter sailing towards me and I signalled with my shirt and screamed at the top of my voice. I should have remained silent. The men in the boat were working for a family called the Caulkers. They wrestled me on to their boat and sailed off to Bunce Island with me as their prize. On that island they have what they call a factory. A slave factory. It's where people are turned into property. I saw things I can never tell you, my brothers and sisters. And I became something I should never have become.'

'You were made a slave?' asked the Jamaican.

Patrick laughed. 'A slave! No, worse. Much worse than a slave. Being a slave wouldn't have given me these grey hairs, this limp, it wouldn't have aged me like this. No, I was not a slave. I was made a slave-driver. A slave-maker. They saw that I was an educated young man, that I could read, write, and knew some languages of the Europeans and the people of the interior as well. They realized I could keep accounts and build trust, rapport, develop custom and bring in business, just the way my father had taught me. They saw that in me and chose not to sell me, but to use me within the factory to grade, order and classify the people prior to their sale.'

'You were a slaver?'

'I was not. I was as much a slave as any I put up for sale. I had no name, I was their property. I could move nowhere unless so ordered by my masters. But I ate well and my bed was a pallet alone, not a soiled stone floor with several dozen strangers.'

'Did you not encourage others to their freedom?' the preacher asked.

'Others, no. They would not have known what to do, where to go, where they were. *I* tried to escape. After a period of some months they started to trust me with the care and transport of letters of credit, introduction and safe passage, and even large sums of money.'

'And so you ran?'

'Yes. I took my chance one day when we were travelling past the inlets up by Guinea. A place I knew well. I got away and managed to stay on the run for three days, but they had dogs and I was caught, beaten and brought back. They did this to me.'

I looked away as he lifted the eyepatch.

The crowd shouted: 'Shame!'

'And so I stayed with them for a long while,

becoming one of them. Thinking like them. Feeling like them. Almost living like them. But the fire of freedom had been lit in my belly. At last, I was given the task of walking some slaves the last stretch of a journey to the coast of Guinea. I murdered my associates with the help of the slaves, and as a body we walked to Freetown and to freedom.

'But by then it was too late. My father was dead. The house was gone and all I knew was that my two brothers' he indicated Robert and me 'all the family I had left in the world, were here in London. I signed on as a landsman on a Plymouth-bound packet-boat and jumped ashore and ran for it as soon as we docked. And here I am.'

I realized I was crying. I had never cried like that before. My tears and sobbing would not stop. I cried for everything; for Patrick, for Robert, for myself, for Father and Mother, for Sierra Leone. Then I was crying for our people in the Americas and the Caribbean, for the poor black wretches of Whitechapel, Wapping and East Smithfield who were stuck here for ever, never to see their homelands again. They were the people I had earlier despised. And I was now one of them. That day I realized I was crying for everybody in the world with a black skin.

And I finally wept for my father: a great man whose passing did not even merit the smallest notice in an English newspaper.

Through my tears, I saw Patrick. His eyes brimmed with tears, but he was smiling at me. He had our father's smile.

Time started again.

[25]

Later that Sunday, back at The Shovel, the three of us sat together as brothers. I joined them in a toast of a very nasty-flavoured spirit which Patrick promised would 'bite back at the cold'. It did.

'I thought I . . . I thought I had . . .'

'You thought you had killed me. I know.' Patrick put an arm on my shoulder. 'And you never told Father the truth about it, did you?'

'Although I had put that little puzzle together a long, long time ago,' pipped Robert.

'I feel no ill will towards you, Jupiter. You were not to have known how that day by the waterfall would unfold.'

'I should have jumped in after you. I could have saved you.'

'Impossible, there is the devil's own current in that river,' Robert added. 'You would both have swirled to your doom.'

I flashed him a glare, and angled myself across the table by way of cutting him out of the discussion.

'Tell me again how Father died.'

'They came by night up the Bullom shore. About a hundred of them. Maybe pirates, maybe not. They had cannon offshore and cannon onshore with them as well. Father, as a man of affairs, was a target. Some say the attack was made to get him alone. Just a way to control his business. I don't know. I wasn't there. I was in another place along the coast when all that happened.'

I could not believe him. Father was known throughout Sierra Leone and in London too. There would have been news of his death in the newsheets, surely. Robert spent all his money on them and would surely have come across such news. I should have known before anyone else.

I declined Patrick's offer of another drink and asked another question: 'How did he die?'

'Shot. A ball to the heart by all accounts. Died cleanly, with cutlass in hand.'

'So he fought to the end. Good.'

'The house was ransacked and burnt to the ground. They even took all the books away with them.'

'So we have no home to return to?'

'Correct.'

'And what of the business?'

'There is none.'

'And the family fortune?'

Robert rounded on me with more rage in his face than he had ever presented before. 'Jupiter! Patrick is trying to tell you something. We are alone here. Our father has been killed. We have no money back home. If we escape from this mess we'll be lucky if we even get back home. And once we do, we'll have to make our own way like the poorest of the poor. We are in trouble. We are paupers. Our name no longer carries any weight. Do you understand?'

'What are you talking about, Robert? We are not paupers! Where did the money come from to buy your clothes? On what money do we live in this place? And what of the money I gave to you, Patrick? . . . Patrick?'

They both looked away from me.

'Brothers, what is our situation? Where is our money? My money?'

'Jupiter, we have no money. We needed much more than was in our purse to purchase tickets for our passage back home. I sought to increase our funds. Decided to use the money on games of chance. You may have noticed they are played with some regularity here.'

'I did notice that. I also noticed you both enjoying

the games, but I never thought . . . my own brothers.' They still refused to meet my gaze. 'And as we are paupers, do we now support ourselves through your petty crimes and associations?'

'A little,' said Patrick, 'but mainly, we are in debt.'

'I thought these people were your friends, Patrick? You must have some influence here. They respect you.'

'They respected my money, while I had it.'

The crew at The Shovel were not exactly the 'bucko mates' Patrick had described. He had, in fact, been living on credit and the sufferance of the landlord for well over a month now. Our arrival improved his situation only briefly. I found a bill under my sackcloth bedsheet. It had been left by the cook. It amounted to four pounds' worth of lodging, food and drink.

I started the week with a desperate plan.

'I have judged you too harshly, Patrick,' I said. 'I witheld a couple of pounds from you when you demanded Father's emergency money from me. I propose that I use it now to play one of the games in the house. Come now, it makes perfect sense. We are in no position to seek proper work. We have no trades, and none to vouch for us in our present condition. Two pounds is not much at all, and I have always been lucky, have I not?'

They stared at me as if I had lost my mind.

'Have you a better idea?' I screamed.

'I confess, I have no better idea – except to run from here and hide. We must go with your judgement, little brother. But this is something you have to do on your own. I could not bear to watch. You are new to games of chance and, sadly, a gambling man can make more chances than a lucky one.'

Patrick spoke in riddles, but at least I had his assent. I vowed to myself that I would earn his respect that day.

Father would have been appalled to see me in a scene such as that which took place under the roof of The Shovel that morning. I cannot say I did not feel embarrassed as I ascended the stairs to the betting parlour. Instead of putting the last two pounds to our family's name towards some venture requiring industry, thrift and temperance, I was betting on rolls of the dice in a public house on the first working day of the week.

The game was slated to start at ten o'clock. I was the first player to arrive. I waited until eleven o'clock for the others. By the look of them, they had just stepped off ships from foreign parts. I was shocked to see the bets they were offering. One had a caged parrot, another a spyglass, the third a large fistful of coins that contained notes of all lands, from rupees to doubloons. I was the only one holding English money.

I was no fool and I quickly took the measure of my adversaries. Naturally, they sought to take advantage of my youth by offering me drinks of the coarsest kinds. I stuck to saucers of tea. They sought to befriend me with tales of their travels and adventures, but I could see they were not very experienced seafarers and most of their stories were clearly lies and empty boasts. We chatted and waited for the serious gamesmen to turn up. Eventually, at around one o'clock that afternoon, a group of four African sailors arrived. All wore the most extraordinary tattoos on their faces. They glittered with jewellery of all kinds. They had just been paid off from a ship and were keen to start spending their money. They ordered wine for all and immediately opened a game of Crown and Anchor.

I passed both my notes to the banker and nodded my wish to join the game. Others soon warmed to the dice-play and before they rolled there was over ten pounds banked. The betting started off fairly low, with players looking for only one of their numbers to come up.

I was not so cautious. I had come to swell my purse. When my turn came at the cup, I declared that I would throw for three crowns, thus trebling my two pounds stake. I was more surprised than anyone else when my prediction proved accurate and three crowns rolled face up on to the mat. I returned my winnings to the bank and waited for the dice to pass around again. The rest of the room was struggling to hold on to their money or was slowly losing it, but I knew I would leave that room richer than I had entered it.

Have you ever felt absolute certainty? When I say that, I mean have you ever felt for a moment as if the world is under your control? Well, for me the world was that smelly little room and all the people, things and events happening in it. I felt like I was drawing all light, heat and luck unto myself. It was as if the other players were there only to watch me take their money.

The cup came round to me. I shook it, this time betting on three kings. The dice rolled true: three kings and eighteen pounds were mine.

The sailors were silent now. They withdrew their money from the game. All except one. He placed the spyglass before me. It was a beautiful instrument. I could see it was a thing of excellent craftsmanship and ingenuity.

'Pure gold,' he whispered. 'The purest.' He passed his hand over it in reverence. 'It was once owned by a prince of Sind. A wise man. A great astronomer.'

'Is this your stake in the game, sir?'

He bowed as if ashamed and reached for the cup. He declared for three hearts. He rolled and got them.

I had to get three crowns or anchors on my throw, or I would lose everything.

I threw a club, a diamond and an anchor.

[26]

'A spyglass? It is a telescope, to be precise, Jupiter,' Robert insisted.

'But look at it! It's worth a fortune. It was owned by a prince of Sind.'

'Sinned against, don't you mean?'

'But Patrick, look closely. This object is made of the purest gold. We can sell it!'

Robert snatched it from me, turned it over a few times and scratched at a join. 'You are correct. It is of the purest gold: the purest gold paint!' He bashed it against a standpipe.

'And *how* much did you lose against this? Was it more than the four pounds we owe the house? It was, wasn't it? How much? Five pounds? More? Ten? No, Jupiter – please, please, I beg you, no more than ten. It was, wasn't it?'

They held their heads in their hands and groaned.

'We are lost!'

Robert turned away from me and started with his *Jupiter, stupider, Jupiter, stupider, Jupiter, stupider . . .*

I swung at him. Patrick caught my hand and held it firmly. 'Never hit that boy,' he hissed.

'But he insulted me. He forgot himself. It is my duty as his older brother to correct him.'

'As it is my duty to correct *you*, young Jupiter. Robert will not be struck again.'

I realized in that moment that he was right. Robert would not be struck. At least not by me. But Patrick would be. He most certainly would be!

I could not bear to remain another second in that house. I ran on to East Smithfield carrying the collapsed spyglass in my bag. The street was utterly run down and smelt of human waste. What had seemed delightful a few nights before now appeared hideous in the light of day. The area east of the Tower was home to thousands of drunk men, drunk women and their drunken children. Drunkards were lying face down in the street. Clubs of drunkards sat on walls, in parks, gardens and street corners playing cards. Drunkards sang singly and together, sometimes the same song. There were even drunkards on horseback and dancing drunkards. And everybody in London looked mad: that mixture of fierceness and dullness that crosses even the kindest faces here several times a day; the look I could summon all too easily myself now.

'The fairest city in all creation!' Father had called London, yet he must have walked these rough, rutted tracks with their rows of subsiding houses. Almost every house was built from bent timber, and he would surely have recoiled at how no object was laid straight with another. I walked down entire streets without glass.

I had never felt such violent rage as coursed through me at that moment. I bowled mindlessly through the streets, without making way for women. I barged into men, daring them, wanting them to take offence. I felt mad enough to challenge the whole of East London. If I returned to The Shovel, I believe I would have killed my brothers. Who were they to treat me like that? Regardless of my errors, I had only been trying to restore our fortune. I was to be praised, not mocked. They were no longer of any concern to me. How they made their way in this world was no longer my business.

Before I knew it, I was at the waterfront. The sight of all those ships (some of them were *majestic*!) filled me with awe and nearly lifted my anger. Just the smells of cinnamon, spilt wine and rotting fruit, mingled with the curses of the dock workers and seamen, almost took me away from my troubles. I sat on a step to take it all in. So many sails, so many destinations. Cargoes of tea, spices, furniture, Chinese porcelain and jade, and jewellery. All non-English names sounded wonderful to me: *Tahiti – Rotterdam – Livorno – Paramaibo – Bencoolen . . . Freetown, Sierra Leone*!

It would be easy for a strong, useful young man such as myself to sign aboard a ship. I knew ropecraft, could cook and work wood well enough. I had some small knowledge of sailing. There were always ships readying to leave for west Africa. Money wasn't necessary, I could work my passage and be home in a few weeks' time if I was lucky. But I would have to be very careful indeed in my choice of vessel. I knew all too well that much of the business transacted on that coast was the trade in people like myself.

Choosing a ship was simpler than I had imagined. The slave ships were all too easy to identify. They stank. It was a stink unlike any I had ever known. Even when it had been washed down with quicklime it still hit you. It smelt worse, in fact, like covering over the traces of a crime. It smelt like all the madness of torture and shame had seeped into the timbers and floated free in the air about those ships like a mantle.

Slave ships shimmered with malevolence.

I headed east, looking up at the ships as I walked, as if I was shopping for the ideal transport. I asked along the docks about vessels likely to be heading off to Africa. Everyone I spoke to regarded me very strangely. Eventually I was directed to a scruffy little office beside a ship's chandler. The fellow behind the counter didn't even look up from his papers when I entered.

'Good afternoon, sir. My name is—'

'Don't worry about your name now.' He continued to scratch at his work. 'When are you looking to be sailing?'

'As soon as possible, sir.'

'Don't "sir" me. You'll be sir-ing enough when you get on board. Have you sailed before?'

'I know coastal navigation and river and inlet work. I can work as a pilot in such waters.'

'Let's see your hands!'

He nearly jumped from his chair when I brought my hands into view. He sat up, rearranged his clothes and adjusted his spectacles. 'I take it you have sailed aboard a merchant or navy ship before?'

I shook my head.

'I'm afraid I can offer you no work, young man.' He stood to shoo me from the room. 'We have work only for subjects of His Majesty, such as need it.'

'I am a subject of the King!' I declared. 'I am willing and able-bodied, and I wish to work a passage on board a vessel travelling to West Africa. To the settlement at Sierra Leone, to be specific.'

'Any vessel?'

'Sir, I am most eager to travel, but I am *not* a fool.'

He sat down again and summoned me forward. 'West Africa . . . let's see now.' He flicked through a huge series of ledgers and timetables, licking his fingers for each page. 'You might be lucky, young . . . what did you say your name was?'

'My name is Ju— Julian, sir. Julian Temba.'

'You may be lucky, Julian. There are not many English sailors who would volunteer for the Africa trades. You can be off the coast there for months at a time, as I'm sure you know. The fever strikes down the white man in great numbers over there. We certainly don't get many hands wishing to return. Unless they're slavers, that is!'

He laughed a single laugh: *Ha!*

'Ah, here we are. The ship's called the *Gadfly*, a merchantman. They're signing on hands right now. I'll recommend you to the bosun's mate.'

'Will I not speak with him before we set sail?'

'He will meet you here. Might ask you a question or two. Might not. If he likes you, you follow him on. He trusts me, see. I've been matching hands to ships for a long time, and I'm never far wrong. This office isn't for your regular seamen, as you may have gathered. It's more for those who don't exactly have professional reasons for wanting to leave the country, if you get my meaning?'

'I do, sir.' My lying was improving. I did not have the vaguest idea what he was talking about.

'You're not running from anything in London town, are you, Julian?'

'Why sir, I am not!' I said, feigning indignation.

'Not that I'd worry myself too much if you were. You look like a good lad all the same, and I'll do my best to see you are sorted with a berth on the good ship, *Gadfly*.' He returned to his work.

'Why, thank you, sir!'

'You have another question for me?'

'Sir, the *Gadfly*. She is not a slaver, is she?'

'What do you take me for, boy? How dare you insinuate such a thing! Putting a young negro to toil on a slave ship? I am insulted.'

He didn't look very insulted, but I asked his forgiveness and a final question: would the good ship

Gadfly perhaps be in need of two further hands – one an experienced sailor?

'If they are people of your calibre, Julian, I will vouch for them with the bosun's mate. The ship weighs anchor at nine o'clock tomorrow evening. The bosun's mate will meet you here at eight.'

To allay my fears that it was not a slaver, I walked half a mile further downriver to inspect it. There was nothing about the *Gadfly* to make the sensitive weep. The vessel seemed well made and clean. Not like a slave ship at all. A goodly number of guns on two decks ringed the ship for a start. The only odours were of salt-caked sails, scrubbed timber and bilgewater. Accordion and fiddle music was playing somewhere below decks and a couple of voices – clear and well modulated – called to one another from the masts. This looked like a jolly ship and a clean ship. Tomorrow it would be *my* ship. I saluted the figures in the rigging. They returned the salute.

I could have jumped for joy.

I dawdled on the way back to the pub. I would let them wait for me, grow anxious and, ultimately, regret their unfeeling treatment of me. I imagined my entrance. They would, at first, try to hide their joy at my return. Then when I told them (in unhurried tones) about the *Gadfly*, and of how we could be back in Sierra Leone within weeks, they would be unable to contain their excitement. As I strolled amongst those extraordinary docks, I rehearsed how I would accept their apologies; how I would suggest they order their affairs prior to leaving The Shovel without paying. They would listen to me and follow me now, for I would be their leader (in a quiet, assured way, of course).

I was in no hurry at all now. It was already dark. I broke my journey by the Ratcliffe docks and leant against a wall overlooking the Thames, that beautiful river of dreams that would carry us back home! I whipped out the spyglass and extended it. I loved the way the furthest details first shot into view. It was shocking at first, but after a while the feeling that I could reach out, pick up and manipulate all these people like dolls was very calming. I studied the buildings and docks of Rotherhithe on the opposite bank. It seemed very busy, but the volume of traffic on the water made it difficult to observe for any length of time. A squadron of Royal Navy frigates was sailing past into Deptford. I soaked up every magnified image from the rigging to the berth decks and gun decks. Everyone on deck looked suitably lively, and my attention was especially taken by the sight of the handful of young black boys like myself who were manning the rigging and trotting around hauling duffel bags and generally looking sharp.

During my period of abandonment at The Shovel, I often heard stories about the accomplishments of our people in His Majesty's Navy. The stories sounded ridiculous to me. Our family owned several properties in Freetown where English sailors stayed, but I had only ever met white men there. At The Shovel I heard old African sailors tell of black midshipmen, black surgeons, and even of a black man captaining a white crew in one of His Majesty's vessels. I still did not believe any of this, but looking at the crews on deck and on land, it was clear that a good many of our people were employed in this service. My spirits were now fully restored.

Because my mouth had been wide open in wonder, the knuckle of the hand that suddenly silenced my screams was actually in my mouth. It was a gritty, grotty hand. I could taste old tobacco, ale, sweat and all kinds of lifelong grime which it is better not to recall, let alone describe. But I think you understand what I'm trying to say. Have you ever bitten a dirty door knob? I mean really crunched down hard on one with your front teeth, as if you are trying to bite an apple. And I'm not talking about a wooden or even a brass door knob, but one made of marble, that you may as well lick for all the difference teeth will make to it. Well that was what that fist in my mouth was like. Solid.

I said: '*Ngwarargh!*'

The person who owned the fist said: '*Hurk-urk-urk*', which I realized was laughter. Laughter of a kind I remembered. I was spun around to face my captor. It was Bavya. Then I saw his bunched fist (which I also remembered from before). It was the last thing I remembered again.

[27]

My feet were bare.

Raucous singing and the clanking of pewter mugs could be heard somewhere beyond the darkness. I tried to raise my head and felt the weight of rough, damp material pulling it back. My head was stuck. I touched around it and realized it was attached to a canvas sheet with my own drying blood. I felt like I needed to pass water, but I couldn't. There were knots in my stomach from a fear so strong it had attacked me during sleep. It attacked me now. I was in absolute blackness. Everything was damp. When I lifted my hand to clear my nostrils, an uncontrollable dread took hold of me. I struggled to turn my mind from facing what I feared had befallen me.

What had I done?

If only I hadn't stormed away from my brothers. Why couldn't I just get along with people like everyone else? Apart from my brothers, there was nobody in the world who would care where I was tonight. And what were Patrick and Robert feeling right now: regret or relief? Perhaps the boys at the academy were wondering how I was doing, but would one of them shed a tear if they heard I'd been murdered or found floating in the Thames? I think not. They would say maybe: *diddums*. Some would rejoice.

I started to whisper the Lord's prayer. After the sixth verse, my breathing became more shallow, if no more regular. The most important thing was not to panic. I knew if I lost my mind in there it would be lost for ever. The instant my verses ended, I felt the fear return with added power. I started going through every Biblical verse I could recall. Lucky for me that Father also had an active ministry and he had literally beaten entire sections of God's word into me. After the Psalms, my stock of verses was drying up. So I began to sing. I sang *Come, let us to the Lord our God.* I have so often been told that mine is not a singing voice that I know it is true. What I had no idea of was that my singing could instill the fear of God into others.

Someone screamed, and chains rattled very close to me in the darkness. I screamed and scuttled away from the sound as fast as I could. The other person in the darkness screamed even more loudly and thrashed like a maniac in their chains. To mask my fear I turned my scream to a roar. I roared so loudly I scared myself. I roared until my voice was hoarse and there was no other noise. I listened closely to the silence. There was a new noise. It was very quiet, very controlled and very definitely laughter.

Unable to contain myself, I sprang across the room in the direction of the sound and grabbed wildly. I was grabbing armfuls of air. The laughter continued only more loudly.

'Who is there?' I called.

'Oh. It's *you*!'

The voice was young and well-spoken. The voice was familiar, but I have no memory for people. 'Who is there? Who are you? Step forward!'

'Hello – Jupiter, isn't it? Strange that we should meet again like this, don't you think?'

'Step forward. Give me your name!'

'It is you who must step forward, Jupiter. I am chained and cannot move freely. Here . . . here I am. Over here.'

I moved towards the rattling chains until I was close enough to hear his breathing.

'It's *me*, Jupiter!'

The slap across my face which followed was all the harder for being unexpected. I reached over to choke the wretch, but he was prepared for my assault and I suddenly found my forearms wrapped in his chains. He tried to turn and throw me over his shoulder. This was his mistake. Although he was a fast and clever fighter, he was somewhat shorter than I was. I would not be thrown, and soon had the boy by the neck in a firm headlock.

'Now just tell me who you are or I'll break your neck!'

'Francis,' he gurgled.

'Francis? Francis who?'

'I have no other name. Just Francis. Don't you remember me?'

I couldn't place him.

'At Mr Thornton's house. You slapped me by way of saying farewell.'

I loosened my grip instantly. I knew it was wrong of me to have struck the child when I left Thornton's mansion, but he irritated me enormously. I did not know if I could handle being cooped up with him for very long, but we were both prisoners and a truce of some sort was necessary.

'Francis,' I said, giving him my hand. 'You were right to avenge yourself. I slighted you grievously. I hope we can work together in trust and friendship.'

'I hope so too, Jupiter!'

'Do you know where we are, young Francis? Tell me this is not a slave ship!' I clutched at him like a lunatic.

He shrugged me away. 'This is no slaver. Have your senses left you so completely?'

'What do you mean by that?' I rose to a crouch, ready to fight him again if his insolence continued.

'I mean our walls are of stone, not wood. Can you hear creaking timbers? Can you feel or hear water, or our prison's movement in it?'

He was right, of course. Fear had driven reason from me. 'Then what place is this?'

'If the sign I saw as they brought me in is correct, this place is known as The Crown and Sceptre. We are in the cellar.'

'The Crown and Sceptre! On the Roman Road?'

'The same.'

The darkness in that space suddenly felt like the darkness of the grave. It might as well have been a slave ship for all the hope I had of surviving it. Waves of panic threatened to engulf me, but I had to be strong, not just for myself but for Francis, who appeared unaware of the fate which awaited him.

'And what brings a nice, cheerful, obedient little chap like you to such a place, Francis?'

'Well, it's all your fault, really.'

'How so?'

'When you walked into the house with Mr Thornton, talking to him as an equal almost, it made me think of my own position. You looked like the sort of young gentleman I'd see myself as being some day. I wondered who you could be and where you came from.'

'I only came from across the Common. You know, from the African Academy.'

'The what?'

'Don't you know of the African school in Clapham?'

'I know nothing whatsoever of Clapham. My duties confined me to the house.'

'I thought as much. How long have you served Mr Thornton?'

'Some two years, but he is a good master,' he said, perhaps sensing my shock. 'He doesn't beat me.'

'Then who, pray tell, does?'

'One of the footmen. All the footmen, in fact.'

'And where were you going when you escaped?'

'I had no idea, Jupiter. I sought only freedom with others of my kind. You showed me that such people existed.'

'Well, you have found me, which is something, I suppose. How far did your travels take you?'

'I walked across the common land to a road. There was a sign for London – said it was no more than three miles distant. I started to walk with a brisk step. After a while I came to another village – Stockwell, I believe. A wagon drew up alongside me and the driver motioned me to enter. Apart from the villainous footmen, I had known nothing but good of the English. I joined him in his wagon and he brought me here. That was two days ago.'

'What did he look like?'

'He was a large man. A very large man. I don't think he is an Englishman, perhaps that accounts for his badness.'

'Did you recognize his language?'

'He spoke not a word.'

'Bavya. You'll come to know him well, soon enough. Was there anyone else with him?'

'He travelled alone.'

I sensed him tembling. His sniffles and tears came soon after. I could not say I was fond of the lad, but we were in this hell together. I was duty-bound to cheer him up. Sooner or later they would be coming for one or both of us and we had to keep our minds away from that fact.

'Tell me something of your life, boy.'

He settled back down into his shackles. After a while, his weeping subsided and he replied: 'I know not where I was born, but I have been told I was brought to this country while still an infant. England is all I know. I have no other home. I used to live with an old couple in another very grand house in a part of London that was set on hills. It had very grand views.'

'What did you do in this house? What were your duties?'

'Duties? I had none. I dressed well. I ate well. Sometimes I went with the lady of the house to the theatre or on visits to her other old lady friends. They liked to touch my hair, but mostly they were kind. They died, the old couple. They were blown over a cliff by a strong wind. I was there when it happened.' He was laughing again. A good sign. 'It wasn't funny, really, but they did both scream like babies, and the old man farted the loudest and longest fart I've ever heard as they were blown away.'

'Yet you were saved. How was this?'

'They did not really like me to wander freely outside the house, a bit like Mr Thornton, I suppose. I was made to remain in the carriage. I was chained to it. Chained at the collar. When their property was disposed of, none of their children wanted me and Mr

Thornton was kind enough to take me in.'

He started crying again. It was clear he had never had occasion to speak about his life before. He had never been amongst his own people. He had never made acquaintance of anyone his own age.

My own banked tears would have compounded his own had it not been for the turning of a key in the lock.

Father once told me how to spot evil. True evil, he said, is never theatrical. It does not declare itself. It does not appear in a flash of lightning in a velvet cloak hissing '*At last we meet!*' There is no hooved, horned man living in the bowels of the earth. And he does not have a tail, nor does he eternally prod unbelievers with a fiery trident. No. Evil must always try to be normal. Evil is that person trying hardest to fit in: that person trying to be the most like everyone else. Look for those who stand behind the shouters and ranters. Watch out for the person most like you or me, who offers no opinion yet is always at the centre of things, he said. Look for those with fixed half-smiles.

When the door opened I was almost disappointed not to see Bavya. The man standing in the light was flanked by two stouter fellows standing a pace or so behind him. He was nondescript in every way except for his colour. He was oatmeal all over. His skin, eyes, hair, even his lips were the colour of oatmeal. He spoke in some impossibly flat and slurred English regional dialect.

'Let's be 'avin yer then. No, not you, shorty. You, big lad!'

My father had told me something else about the evil ones. Someone like Bavya was visibly crazed, lonely and broken, and as such it was in my power to understand him and, if I chose to, I could pity him, and, one day if I was strong enough in Christ, I could even forgive him. Perhaps. But I could see I was now in the clutches of one who went home every night and bounced his children on his knee and who stood in his family pew every Sunday. Someone who looked as if he could wipe last night's blood off his shoes every morning before going down to eat his porridge. Just a normal man doing an everyday job of tearing human souls apart.

[28]

The merrymaking in the pub's main room stopped abruptly the moment I was shoved over the threshold. There were upwards of twenty men in that pub. Every one of them looked as if they wanted to kill me. I stared down the uglier ones, but some of the company wore such refined, experienced and composed expressions that I felt my bowels begin to loosen. One of the ugly faces was Bavya's. One of those composed expressions was worn by Mr Unwin. He shouldered his way forward. He shook his head at me.

'You really have no idea how much trouble you have caused, do you, Jupiter? Did you not think we'd find you? Did you not see you'd stand out? Have you no sense? Little twinkletoes. Little shiny shoes,' he whispered. 'The school and its governors are in quite a state. Clapham has never seen anything like it. Mr Wilberforce, Mr Sharp, Reverend Venn, all of them – and you should see Mr Thornton these days: white as a sheet, he is. He has taken the responsibility for your disappearance upon himself. As well he should. There has even been talk of closing the school. As for my associates here, well, let's just say they have been discomfited by your behaviour. But you must forgive me, I'm talking about these gentlemen as if they were not present.'

He nodded to the two stalwarts who accompanied Oatmeal-face. They held me firmly by the arms.

'I really should introduce them properly. Bavya, of course, you know of old. I believe you've also met Mr Philips, no?'

The skinny little man I had batted around the cellar when I rescued Robert walked up to me. His head was bandaged. He spat in my face and punched me in my stomach. I doubled up. I was not in as much pain as it appeared. I was hoping to appeal to their nobler instincts: the sight of a young person in agony would staunch their anger. I was unsuccessful.

'Mr Cox, too, has already made your acquaintance.'

I froze. Mr Cox was the fellow I had attacked with Reverend Wilde's poker. The brute had survived. And he was carrying the same poker. He waved the fire-tool before my eyes and stabbed the air around my face.

A hand darted out and held his wrist. 'Put that away. I'll use metal on the boy. That's my job, for later,' said Oatmeal-face. He patted me on the back as if this news could comfort me.

'There'll be no later after I've finished with him,' said Mr Cox.

'One swing and one alone, Mr Cox. And not too hard, mind. We still need to get a price for him to make up for the loss of his brother.'

Mr Cox's belly-blow *did* hurt. It knocked me off my feet. I was gasping for breath and was doubled over for a while.

I thanked God that my next assailant was Mr Unwin. His punch was as feeble as I expected, but coming in the wake of Cox's fist it hurt more than it should have.

Oatmeal-face hauled me up by the collar. 'He's mine to mark. Mine to mark, lads! No blades, no cudgels, no flames. This blackamoor is mine to mark! You each have one swing and one alone. Use it well. And no marking!'

I was lifted on both sides and flung into that mass of howling bullies. They called it 'running the gauntlet'. I was meant to charge between two rows of them. The idea was that every man would try to connect a single boot or fist.

It was not like that, of course. It was a free-for-all. My face was smashed times beyond number. The rapid succession of blows to other parts of my body made me lose all sensation. They tore at me like starving wolves. Those who could not get near enough to lay hold of me fought their friends to do so. I was stamped on, kneed, elbowed and headbutted by an unrelenting army of madmen. My muscles were so dead and stiff I could not even raise my arms in self-defence. At one point I saw myself floating above the scene, watching my body being knocked back and forth, back and forth. Very soon my head wound reopened. I knew teeth were being dislodged. Blood filled my mouth and I could no longer breathe without vomiting. But I would not cry. I would not scream out. No matter how bad it got, I would never cry. I just thanked God that my father was dead. He would never have to live in the knowledge that a son of his had been beaten by white men.

I was almost grateful when Bavya's unmistakeable wobbling fist swung round to knock me out.

[29]

When I came back to my senses in the cellar, I realized to my horror that the thugs upstairs had merely been playing with me. They could have killed me if they had really wanted. They could have wounded me much more severely than they had, but they knew a broken black boy would stay an unsold black boy.

My face was being mopped by Francis. A torn strip of his shirt served to stem the flow of blood from my forehead. He was weeping. I imagined I looked a lot worse than I felt. Even though I could not see him in the darkness, I turned my face away from him. 'I have shamed my father's memory,' I muttered.

'Your father!' Francis spoke the word as if he could not comprehend it. 'Tell me about him. Please, Jupiter, tell me about your father.'

I imagined my father standing in front of me wearing his church clothes. He was nodding and smiling at me. The image cleared my mind and settled my spirits. I felt compelled to talk.

'My father and mother were born into slavery in

America. They died as free people in Africa. It was where they both always wanted to die, they said. My family are . . . we were important people in Sierra Leone. Every day our house would be visited by kings, traders, ships' captains. All sorts of people. It was a nice life.'

'What was your house like?'

The boy was clearly hungry for details of a life he had never possessed. I felt the strain in his questions. It was as if he needed this information from me before one of us died.

'Which house? We had many houses. Our main place was in Westmoreland Street in the middle of Freetown. There were other smaller houses, five or so, dotted around town, but they were rented out to various parties and we only ever saw them from the outside. Then we had the two properties upcountry. They weren't really houses at all. They were actually wooden stockades. Everything we needed for our journeys could be found there: medicines, weapons and supplies. We spent a lot of time at those places. When we weren't there, they were home to some of our trusted employees, their families and friends. Lastly there was the house at Bureh Beach which we used for fishing weekends, entertaining.'

I told Francis all about the parties that we held there. I had forgotten how it all was: the food, the music, the sunsets. I must have spoken for hours. The next thing I knew Francis was snoring away and his head bounced once on my shoulder. I managed to shift him on to his bed of rags and let him sleep on.

I hoped I had given him something to dream about.

Breakfast was mashed turnips with lumps of pork fat, and ale. The cellar door was left open to give us light to eat with. The food was cold and the drink tasted as if a toad had died in it. I ate and drank all, however, and asked for more. I ate that as well. Halfway through my second pint, I felt my aches and pains from the previous night ebbing away, but the taste was making me nauseous and I could drink no more. Francis ate nothing, but he drank a full three pints of ale, like a true English boy, with no ill-effect. His burp of appreciation brought one of the heavy-set boys. 'I sincerely hope you enjoyed that, littl' un. Could well be the last ale you have for a long time.'

Oatmeal-face came to see us with a strange-smelling man whom he referred to as 'Dr Barrymore'. After this man had tapped our heads, peered into our mouths, and pulled our arms about, I had no better idea which branch of medicine he was qualified to practise. He asked me if I was in any pain at all. I told him I was in agony throughout my body and had been for every hour of my sleepless night.

'Interesting,' he sniffed. 'This one needs to be in sunlight. Keep him in an upstairs room. This damp will ruin him. Give him a cup of very hot feverfew tea.' He sloped over to look at Francis. 'This one's perfectly fine. Remove his shackles and rub his joints with pork fat and honey. He also needs light and fresh air.'

All the time, Oatmeal-face was following behind him with a scowl. 'Feverfew tea, you say? Pork fat and honey, you say?' He signalled for the 'doctor' to be led from the cellar. 'You can take your payment from the counter!' he shouted after him. 'Pork fat and honey, indeed! Follow me, you two.'

He brought us to an upper room. Our more obvious bloodstains were wiped away and we were commanded to change from our soiled clothes into two grey gowns that looked like nightshirts. The gowns had not been washed for a considerable time, if ever, and the armpits of my garment were alive with lice. Francis and I were locked together with new rust-free chains. A cracked chamber pot was rolled into the room for us. The door was slammed and a key was turned in it.

I was so overjoyed to see sunlight, even through the tiny, grimy window of that narrow, empty room, that it took me a long while to collect myself and realize what was about to happen. I, Jupiter Williams, would soon be sold as a slave. I had been so close to taking my brothers away from this soggy, miserable country. Everything was in place, and now I had nothing. I would probably be bought by some fat planter as a houseboy. He would call me Pompey, or Scipio, or Caesar and make me dance for him or serve sugared tea to his guests. He might even take me to somewhere truly evil like Jamaica and deliver me unto the tender mercies of his slave-drivers in the fields. If the tales told by the Maroon boys of the Englishmen's wickedness on that island were even half true, then I would have to find some means of escape here and now, even if it meant dying in the process.

In the morning light I saw that Francis looked much younger than Robert. His soft life as a household pet had kept his skin unscarred. He had a trusting expression. He stared up at me like a puppy.

I did not know what to do. It was as if everything I had tried had ended in failure and disgrace.

We stood together at the little window and stared out over the hedges of Bethnal Green for a couple of hours. As last looks at freedom went, it wasn't such a bad picture – as long as you forgot about the dozens of crowded, humid rooms in small streets and ugly, mean, uncomfortable alleys that lay out of sight beyond Roman Road. Birds still sang and the clatter of dozens of hand-looms sounded pleasantly from all points. Children played and men of all ranks walked and rode about the streets. We watched some of them turn down the gravel path of The Crown and Sceptre and enter the house by a door beneath us. There was no typical face to these arrivals. Some were grim, some gay. Some dressed and moved as humbly as country parsons, whilst others dressed like peacocks and made their every gesture and thought an act for public display. Londoners of middling rank and above filed into the stinking pub. These people were the backbone of this city. Its tradesmen, lawyers, successful butchers, showmen and society men.

And they had come to buy me.

[30]

The pub's central room had been transformed into an auction hall. Banks of tiered seating had been skilfully raised around it. More tea and coffee was being drunk than ale and spirits. The buyers were like a theatre audience, just as loud and rude, flapping their programmes and eager to get on with the main event.

Francis and I were dragged downstairs and made to sit in a small space underneath the seats of the crowd. We watched the goings-on from between their feet.

We were not the only goods on sale that day. Before they got to us, bids were invited for a 'country-style oak drop-leaf table with Jacobean-style legs, an oak and mahogany long-case clock, a most admirable carriage and bay horses, fit for a gentleman . . .' The list went on for ever. If our own lives had not been for sale that day, I declare we would have fallen asleep, so tedious were the proceedings. If you had ever seen a parcel of French cloth of various grades being assessed and haggled over by the most concerned parties for two hours, you would truly have comprehended the meaning of eternity. In fact, if you are even capable of imagining such an exchange with any accuracy, I pity you.

At long last, our time arrived. To tell you that we awaited our sale with some impatience is probably the saddest thing I could say, but it was true. If we were being sold, then at least something was happening. At least something was happening to *us*.

We were dragged into that shoddy amphitheatre and unchained to light applause and raised voices. A theatrically-dressed auctioneer motioned me to the centre of the room.

'Gentlemen, I give you this tall, well-made young blackamoor. Strong of arm and quick of tongue, but as you see, he can be brought to heel without too much force. He can handle a horse or a sail, so they say. Can speak to Yankee or Frenchie. Can read or write well enough. As a messenger he is fleet of foot, and he can be trained to wait on table or to perform duties within the house.'

I would love to tell you that I scowled indignantly at that room of people buyers, but with God as my witness, I regret to say that I embodied as best I could the descriptions lavished upon me by the auctioneer.

In truth, the man was not exaggerating my qualities. Was I not alert and skilled in many matters? If I was to be sold, I hoped it would be to a household that would appreciate my abilities. I hoped in vain. Bids were roaring from the most brutish-looking people long before the auctioneer finished his introduction.

'I have ninety pounds in ready money on the young nigger!' One bidder stood to wave a wad of notes.

'And I ninety-five pounds!'

'One hundred pounds says he's mine!'

'One hundred and five pounds for the blackamoor! One hundred and five pounds!'

I had not noticed this bidder before. He wore a red scarf around his neck. So did the younger man with a black eye to his side. It was Freddie Franklin of the sharp-hammer gang and his son, Jack. They did not take their eyes off me.

The auctioneer stood back, folded his arms and let the figure climb.

The figure climbed above one hundred and fifteen pounds.

Reader, my confusion grew. Whilst not wanting to be sold at all under any circumstances, I hoped I would go for a decent price. *I was no ninety-pound nigger!*

'One hundred and twenty pounds I say!' Jack

Franklin stared at me with strong silent hatred.

'I'm hearing one hundred and twenty pounds from the gentleman in the red scarf. Do I hear more for this outstanding negro, for this quality black? Do I hear one hundred and twenty-five pounds? Do I hear one hundred and twenty-two pounds? One hundred and twenty pounds and one guinea? No further bids?'

I looked desperately from face to face, praying for another buyer to surface. Anyone but the Franklins.

There were no other bids.

'I hereby declare this boy sold for one hundred and twenty pounds – going, going, gone!'

Never had I heard such terrible words. I was condemned to life as a slave to a gang of dockside cutpurses. 'I will have him!' had been Mr Franklin's cry. And now I was his, to do with as he pleased.

You are mine. He mouthed the words and pointed at me. His son managed to smirk at me using his eyes alone.

'You will be wanting him burnt now, won't you, sir?' pipped Oatmeal-face.

'I will, and I want it done properly, mind.'

'Sir, I've been cutting 'em and branding 'em for more than twenty years on three continents, I'll have you know. There's no better craftsman than me.'

'Very well then, my man. Lead on.'

'Lead on?'

'We will see to it that our property is marked correctly.'

'As you wish, sir.'

31

Have you ever felt hot? When I say hot, I'm not talking about the weather, although you might understand the sort of heat I mean if you have ever walked slowly over a metal sheet at noon during high summer in Sierra Leone. If you have held your hand inches from the flames of a two-hour-old log fire you will have some idea. The branding room was the hottest space I have ever been in. A brazier overflowing with red-hot coals glowed to one side. A selection of branding irons were heating within it. I was strapped to a bench (a *branding bench* of Oatmeal-face's own design!). I was held fast by the ankles, knees, wrists and elbows. Further ties bound my neck and stomach.

'I've been at this task so long, it's like second nature to me. Now how would you like him? Just burnt, or cut and burnt?'

Oatmeal-face looked from father to son. They looked at each other and chorused: 'Cut and burnt!'

'A wise choice, sirs. I always find that a cut followed by a burn makes a better mark. Heals faster too. Burns can swell, bringing dreadful pus and weeping sores. Puts your slave out of work for weeks, that can. I've seen some awful work, I have. One time in Antigua—'

'To work, man! We are in a hurry,' snarled Mr Franklin. He glanced at his pocket-watch. 'Time is against us.'

'So the name's Franklin, is it?'

'That is correct. Frederick Franklin.'

'Hmm. You'll be wanting an F then.' Oatmeal-face sorted amongst some lettered branding tongs. Two Fs maybe. I have some of those, the good old-fashioned double F.' He twisted the tool deep into the coals. 'Give it five minutes or so to get nice and hot.'

'We must leave with our purchase sooner than that. Use bellows!'

'Of course, sir. I'll get the old bellows going, soon enough. In the meantime, I'll just get the slicing out of the way.'

He unrolled a pack of butchers' blades and selected a small paring knife.

The cut he made in my upper arm was only skin deep and it did not hurt. I was really far too low in spirits to be horrified by this stage.

'Now I want to see you burn him in the wound! Brand the blackamoor in the wound while it's still fresh. Do it!' barked the Franklin boy.

'Patience, young sir, patience.' Oatmeal-face extracted the brand using an old cloth and blew on it a few times. 'Hmm, not too bad. It might just be ready.' He waved it at me. 'This will hurt but for a short while. It's the cut, you see. The blood and the fire work together to make a better seal.'

'I will do the burning,' commanded Mr Franklin.

'You shall not, sir.'

'But I shall.' Mr Franklin grabbed the branding iron from him in a sudden sweeping gesture. 'The boy is mine, is he not?'

Oatmeal-face relented. 'Have your damned double Fs then!' he grumbled.

'That's right, all the Fs right here on this iron.' The glow from it lit up his face like a demon. His eyes glowered at me. They did not look human at all. 'That's F for Freddy, F for Franklin, and F for – fool!'

An ugly hissing sound came from Oatmeal-face's head. Mr Franklin was holding him by his hair with one hand and pressing the brand into his face with the other. Even with the bonds about my neck I manage to shiver my face away from that scene. I heard bubbling, splashing and a half-moan as Oatmeal-face's body collapsed on to the stone floor.

'Now it's your turn, Jupiter! Jack, get that nice little knife again. Look lively now!'

But Jack did not get that nice little knife. He turned around to brandish the nastiest cleaver I have ever seen and ran at me like a fiend. I started to choke from the shock of it all, and my voice failed me. Before I could scream he had cut the straps on my right leg. I kicked frantically towards his face, stamped my foot around to keep them from getting closer.

Jack dodged the kicks easily and stepped beyond them to connect his elbow with my chest. That (and his father jumping in with a few choice blows of his own) stopped me. His bunched fist appeared under my nose. 'You are going to do exactly what I say, you 'orrible little blackie.

'You've wasted enough time. You'll put your clothes on and walk out of here between me and Jack. We must leave this instant. Your brothers are waiting. It's right what they say about you. You are trouble. You can't be told anything. Just do what we say and we'll all get out of here alive.'

He cut the strap at my stomach, then sliced through my remaining straps. Father and son levered me from my torture table into an upright position. I kept an eye on them and they did the same to me as I dressed hurriedly. Then I made the mistake of glancing at what was left of Oatmeal-face. I felt vomit rising in my throat, but I kept it down.

The Franklins walked me out of The Crown and Sceptre like a dog. As we passed through the auction, a few of the buyers even raised their glasses and wished me well with sick smiles on their faces. We stepped around the object of their bidding. It was Francis. I have never seen a more pitiful sight. He looked at me leaving as if I was his last hope of salvation – which I imagine I was. Bids for him were hovering around the eighty-pound mark.

As I stepped out of the door I saw him being shackled anew and being led unsold back to the cellar. The Franklins saw it too. We broke into a run the second we stepped over the threshold. We heard shouting in the cellar from fifty yards away. The door burst open and I heard the crack of pistol shots. I had never heard so much gunfire. A very great many pistol shots. It was as if every man in the pub possessed a firearm. And I was their target as I zigzagged towards the cover of the trees.

'Over here!' It was Patrick. Patrick beckoned us from a gap in the wall of a disused stable. We slipped through the gap as neatly as rats.

I embraced Patrick and Robert. Society stood off to one side. He sneered at me openly. His arms were folded over a loaded shotgun. A rough and lively-looking fire roared on the floor at his feet. There were a number of others in the shed. They were all Englishmen wearing red scarves. Shots were striking the stable and one ball made it through the gap to ricochet around us for half a second.

'Mr Franklin, where is your wagon? Should it not be here by now?' Robert inquired with an authority I'd never heard in his voice before.

'He'll be here soon enough, young un. Right now we must keep these gentlemen at bay.' He pointed to the open ground before the pub and the hedges to its sides. It was steadily being peopled by slow-moving armed men.

'How are those fireballs coming along, Society?' Patrick demanded.

Society reached into the flames, picked up a hot stone with his bare fingers and studied it. 'They're good and ready, Patch.'

'Then we attack!'

'Attack?' I asked.

Patrick handed me a slingshot, pointed at the fire, then to The Crown and Sceptre's thatched roof. 'We'll do this together, you and me. Society and one of the Franklin boys will buy us a few seconds of time and cover with their shotguns. Now get busy. Everything you need is in my bag. I'll fire up first. You follow.'

I squatted down and prepared the fireball. I spooned two hot stones into a bowl and quickly added pitch and a mixture of dried fabric strips. The moment before they burst into flames, Patrick ordered the shotguns to lay down a barrage. As they did so he screamed, 'Now!' I tipped the flaming fireball into his slingshot and he side-skipped outside in a throwing run. My slingshot was ready in a second and I followed in his wake. I ran up parallel to him amidst clouds of gunsmoke. I took aim at the roof and swung the slingshot with all my might. I watched the fireballs soar high and land with tiny explosions on the roof. The flames spread rapidly through the filthy old thatch and soon began licking around the upper storeys of the house.

As the villains poured out of the house, Patrick and I picked them off one by one from behind the shelter of the broken wall.

Robert tapped my shoulder and pointed at a figure exiting the building by a side door and making his way past us, shielded by a hedgerow. It was our old schoolmaster: Mr Unwin. Robert moved to snatch the shotgun from Society. I pulled him back and offered him my slingshot. 'Make it clean. One shot.'

'Clean? Just one shot? This is Mr Unwin we are talking about. Jupiter, times have changed. I have changed.' He declined the weapon and tugged a length of rusty chain from the wall. He flexed it and wound it tightly about his fists. 'This'll do.'

He was away out of the door before I realized what was happening. I was too busy flinging missiles and downing anyone coming out of the front door to notice my dear little brother after he slunk off in a crouch along our side of the hedgerow. I never did find out exactly what he did to our old teacher, nor did I ever ask, but over the next minute and a half I heard several clanks of the chain, a hideous gargling noise, several yelps, an 'omygodnoooooonoooooo!' and some dull thwacks, each followed by a low harsh moan.

'Gentlemen,' Society called, 'the wagon is here. Let us be away!'

Patrick and I got in last with the gunmen, and the wagon clattered away at a terrific pace. I looked out at the blazing public house and allowed myself a quiet cheer. It warmed my heart to see smoke billowing from the roof, burning timbers in its attic rooms and parlours, and best of all to know that those torture chambers, the branding room and cellars, would soon become giant ashtrays. There would be no more black boys for sale in that place, no more—!

Francis! He was still in there! He was still chained up in the cellar.

'Patrick, stop the wagon! Stop this instant.'

'Jupiter, have you lost your mind?'

'No, brother. I must get back to the pub immediately. There's someone still in there.'

'Yes indeed, murderers and slavers looking for our blood. We are not stopping. Haven't you caused enough trouble, Jupiter?'

'Where's he going, Patch?' barked Mr Franklin. 'Remember our bargain. I only said we'd get him out for you. That's what we've done, haven't we? You will still honour your side of the bargain.'

'He isn't going anywhere.' Patrick whipped around to face me. 'What do you think this is? Why do you think we have come here? This is all because of you. You have no idea what this is costing us, have you?'

'I must return. There is a child baking to death in there.'

'Since when did you consider other people, Jupiter?'

'Wait for me here, brother. I'll not be long.' I jumped

out of the bouncing wagon and rolled away across the track.

'This is the last time, Jupiter. The very last time. If you are not back within ten minutes, we go.' He threw a slingshot, a bag of missiles and a loaded pistol towards me.

I followed the smoke trails back to the pub. The fire had not fully taken hold on the ground floor. There was a small crowd gathered at the front door, piling up salvaged goods and stock. There was no sign of Francis.

I loaded my slingshot with a whistler and whipped it strongly and sharply skywards. It came screaming down to crash at the feet of those outside the pub. While it was descending I made my way along the hedge back into the pub through the side door. The house was filling with thick, heavy smoke. I poured a half-empty flagon of ale over my handkerchief and wrapped it over my mouth. As I moved towards the cellar stairs I heard timbers within the structure giving way. A huge chunk of the ceiling in the main parlour collapsed, barely missing me, and adding plaster dust to the mix in the room.

I could only just hear banging downstairs. I pressed my mouth to the door. 'Francis! Can you hear me?' The door was locked.

I heard coughing.

'Francis, this is Jupiter. If you can hear me, stand back away from the door. Stand back!' I cocked the pistol, levelled it at the lock and pulled the trigger. I kicked away the splintered wood and nudged the door open. Francis was curled into a corner. He was under his bed of rags. 'It's me, Jupiter.'

'Jupiter?'

I could hardly hear him above the noise of the burning house. 'Yes, we've got to get out of here. Follow me.'

He could barely move. I dragged him forward and walked him to the stairs. I untied my wet handkerchief and fastened it around his face to ease his coughing. 'Not far to go now, just up these stairs, out of the door then we're free.'

Francis was surprisingly heavy. Unless we ran, we would never make it to the wagon on time. It took a long minute to get him to the door. I was on the point of collapsing from the smoke in my lungs. The others would have left by now. They had done all they could to save me from myself and I had failed them. I could not blame them for abandoning me.

'The horses, Jupiter. They keep horses and carriages down the lane. I saw them when I came in.'

I thought the boy was delirious but his words started to make sense.

'How do we get there, Francis?'

'Along the back wall . . . I think there's a part of it we have to climb over . . .'

I needed no further encouragement. The crowd was still far enough away from the building to give us a blind run to the wall.

I had to push Francis up and over into the stable area. He fell on to the other side with an alarming crunch. I vaulted over. There were no single horses. All the beasts were attached to carriages. So much the better!

I settled Francis into a very fashionable, if unmasculine, cabriolet and instructed him on how to load, ready and use the pistol. Then I gently eased the stable door open a fraction. I took my place beside Francis and snapped the reins about the horses, preparing them for a charge. We burst on to the yard in a flurry of hooves, whoops and whipcracks. I believe we might have run over a couple of people on our charge towards open ground. I worked the pair of horses with all my skill and concentration, and relaxed only when The Crown and Sceptre had once again become a smoky smudge in the sky behind us.

When I looked across to share a victory-laugh with Francis, I noticed a large pair of white knuckles gripping the hood of the cabriolet just beside him. Some madman must have jumped on to the running board and clung on for dear life as we tore away from the yard. Whoever it was was pulling themselves into view.

It was Bavya. He was smiling. He held a knife between his teeth and used his great weight to rock the dainty carriage back and forth.

'Francis.' I motioned at our unwelcome passenger. 'Shoot him.'

The boy shrunk back in his seat and held the pistol at arm's length.

'Pull the trigger now.'

'I can't.'

'Do it!'

The vehicle was spinning wildly in the road by now and looked likely to be overturned at any moment. Bavya casually reached over as if to sit amongst us.

'Shoot. Him. Now.' I said, unable to account for the boy's paralysis.

'I can't, Jupiter. I can't!'

The giant steadied himself with one hand on the cabriolet and took the knife from between his teeth . . .

When the pistol went off, it punched a clean hole through Bavya's cheek. He looked at me and shook his head. Then he buckled away from the carriage and collapsed into the road.

'I have never killed anyone before,' said Francis.

'How do you know he is dead?'

My answer gave him no comfort. I could see the Franklins' wagon lumbering ahead of us, so I charged ahead to catch up and join them on our journey back to the docks.

[32]

'Welcome back, Jupiter,' growled Society. He busied himself unloading the wagon in The Shovel's courtyard.

'Oh, hello, Society. I really must thank you for coming to my aid this afternoon.'

'Do not thank me. Thank your brothers. Have you spoken to them since you got back?'

I had not. I was too busy explaining the affairs of The Shovel to Francis. I was intending to thank Patrick and Robert profusely for their valiant rescue, but I was also readying in my mind my speech outlining our future at sea. It had to be perfect.

'Where are they, Society?'

He flapped his hands. 'They could be anywhere hereabouts. But they'll have no time to see you right now. There's the bargaining to complete.'

'The bargaining?'

'Did you think the Franklins came along just for the ride this afternoon? What do you imagine they were doing there? They are not our friends.'

'I do not understand what you say, Society.'

He paused in his work and looked at me curiously. 'Jupiter, that is the first time I believe I have heard you admit ignorance. You have overturned the business of The Shovel. You have reduced us all to beggary and near slavery and made our enemies our overlords.'

I still understood nothing. I was afraid to understand.

'The Franklins are now our masters. *That* was the price of your rescue. They have been given control of the future of The Shovel. Its business will be in their hands for a while. Your brother, Patrick, had to crawl before them and beg for their help. That's how badly did he need an English face – any English face – to front an entry at The Crown and Sceptre this afternoon. And it is lucky for you that Patrick is popular with those English boys. You are very lucky indeed.'

'But why did The Shovel agree to be taken over by whites? This is costing dearly and is most unfair.'

I was consumed by shame. The memory of my father's words rang loudly: '*You must never let the white man beat you!*'

But I had been beaten. In more ways than one. And I had also caused my people to be beaten.

'The Shovel will lose everything because of me?' I wailed.

'We will lose much, but not all. And we may gain much more in return. Indeed our fortunes may well turn on this change.'

'But I still do not understand.' My voice was somewhere between a whisper and a squeal.

Society sat and invited me to sit also. With his hand on my shoulder, he told me: 'Your brother has offered himself to the Blackgang and The Shovel for a period of one and a half years' service. Depending on the nature and quality of business he manages to bring in, his period of service will shorten or lengthen. Of course the larger part of any profits will end up in Franklin family pockets, but he has shown himself to be a versatile and effective planner in the short time he has been here.'

I could not grasp the meaning of his words. My brother, who had fought to escape from slavery, my brother who had made his way across from Africa to be with us, here in London, my brother had offered himself, sacrificed himself for me. He had given up his freedom in order to slave for others for one and a half years!

I shook away my tears. 'My brother is doing this for *me*? After all the trials I have put him through?'

'Be thankful you *have* a brother, Jupiter, and one

who loves you. You cannot imagine how blessed you are.'

'But for Patrick to do all this for me, I'll have to—!'

'*Patrick!* Jupiter, what are you saying? Patrick is not the one laying down his life for you. It is your brother Robert who will work for us as he has worked so outstandingly over the previous week. It is as he says, you understand so little. *Jupiter stupider* . . . eh? Robert has the brains in your family, Patrick the courage. And what do you have? The body-strength. That won't get you far in this world.'

'But Robert can't stay here! He's a scholar. He has to come home with me—'

'He stays here. He wants to. He has pledged to. Ask him. He likes this life. He's good at it. He's even managed to clear your debts as part of the deal with us and the Franklins. How's that for you? With Robert as part of our crew we can enjoy broader perspectives on life, as a young gentleman such as yourself might say. I'll take you up to see your family in a while. But before I do, I have to ask you one question. Jupiter, you've been here a while now. You've seen how things work between all of us down here. Has it ever occurred to you to wonder who I may be? Exactly what it is that I do?'

I spoke the realization as it dawned on me: 'You are the landlord here, Society. You own The Shovel.'

[33]

Patrick thought we looked wonderful. To my eyes we were perfectly kitted out for a life at sea. The three of us were dressed identically in new short-waisted jackets, thick woollen jerseys, tough, clean gunmetal-grey cotton trousers, and new shoes with double-spiked silver buckles. Robert told us we looked like black customs men and that our fashions were wholly inappropriate for a merchant ship. Patrick, who had been to sea before, told us that we were dressed well enough for service on board a ship of His Majesty's Navy and that any mere merchant vessel would be glad to have us. Society advised us to collect woollen caps once on board as a matter of urgency.

The crew-hiring office was closed when we arrived at twenty minutes to eight that evening. Light rain was falling through a dense fog and we took shelter underneath the awning of a nearby cooper. We felt foolish with our new clothes and duffel bags waiting on that stinking dock. Suppose the broker never arrived? What if there was no ship? Suppose this was all an elaborate trap to whisk us all away for sale in the Indies? It was not unknown. Black men vanished all the time in London.

The broker and the bosun's mate arrived together.

'Are all these bound for the *Gadfly*?' the sailor inquired.

'We are,' I declared in as sailorly a tone as I could muster.

'You told me to expect three, not five, Mr Hibbert.'

'We three go with you, bosun's mate.' Patrick's gesture encompassed me, himself and Francis.

The bosun's mate looked us over. His eyes were full of doubt. 'And what about you two, then?'

'We are here to bid them farewell,' said Society.

'Well you've just done it.' He handed the broker a small purse of money and slapped each of us in turn on the shoulder. 'Come on then, we can't keep the captain waiting.'

'Brothers.' Robert rushed forward to embrace us. 'You will write to me the moment you are back in Freetown, won't you?'

We promised we would.

'I will see you under the Cotton Tree within two years' time. And take care with this one.' He chucked Francis under the chin.

Francis stepped away from him scornfully. 'I can take care of myself, thank you very much.'

'Then go with God, young murderer!' Robert chuckled.

'This is all very nice,' the bosun's mate growled, 'but a ship awaits you. There's work to be done.'

'Then let us go to it!' said Patrick in a voice more sailorly than the bosun's mate.

We shouldered our bags and waved farewell. The last time I looked back I saw only masts in the mist. Robert, Society and London were gone.